"A Foolish Love Story"

A Novel By

Uniquely Lashay

Unique Creations Publications is now accepting

manuscripts from aspiring & experienced authors!

Legal Notes

Unique Creations Publications © 2019

WHAT MAKES YOU UNIQUE:

Reaching for your goals no matter who doubts you is what makes you unique. Not letting this world take your creativity and remaining humble no matter what causes you to stand out. When life gets tough, don't give up, just keep pushing for the stars. The people that shine the brightest are often the ones who have been down the darkest roads.

Synopsis

Carmon Wells is a church-going, good girl. She's been living a great life alongside the lord and her parents for as long as she can remember. Seeing the life everyone around her is living from her best friend, Peaches Greene, to her heartfelt crush, Kane Smart and his best friend J.C. , James Cook, she decides that the church life has caused her to miss out on what it's like to be a normal girl at her age.

At age twenty-one, she makes a life-changing decision to leave home and the church for good. On the other hand, she sees her best friend, Peaches, working at the hottest strip club in Duval—Bottom's up, and she seems to be living it up, so Carmon, of course, wants in.

Carmon is new to this lavish lifestyle and will realize that this life change is a bit more than she bargained for. Finishing school and paying bills aren't as easy as Carmon thought it would be. Will she get the life she's out in the streets looking for?

Being foolishly in love with shiny things, you have to be careful what you ask for because everybody can't handle what they might get.

Introduction

I sat there on my sofa waiting for Kane to enter my apartment door like he always did once I got off from the club. He hated that I became a dancer, but it was the only way I could get away from my parents. I needed to be able to provide for myself so that Kane and I could fully be together. Two hours had passed, but still no Kane. Where the fuck could this nigga be? He knew I had school in the morning, so I didn't know what was taking him so long. After a long night at the club, all I wanted to do was see my man. That's when I heard a knock at the door. I jumped up from my living room sofa and rushed to open the door. I just knew it was my boo, Kane, but I didn't understand why he didn't just use his key I had made for him.

"Where have you been?" I asked as I opened the front door. After opening the front door, the first thing I noticed was Kane bent over holding his stomach. I could see blood dripping, but I wasn't sure where it was coming from.

"Help me get inside," Kane said in a demanding voice. I could tell by the way that he said that he was in pain, and he had been shot.

"Bae, what happened to you?" I asked Kane, trying to get clarification.

"Some lame ass niggas shot me," Kane said as I helped him onto my sofa. Kane was leaking so much blood, and by now, my hands were drenched in his blood.

"We have to get you to the ER, Kane. If not, you're gonna die. You losin' too much blood," I replied as I stood over him panicking because I had never seen no shit like this in my life. He looked up at me with tears in his eyes. "I just want you to know, I love you, Carmon," Kane said as he coughed up more blood.

"Kane, please stay with me!" I screamed as I picked up the phone with blood all over my hands and called my best friend, Peaches. If anybody knew what to do right now, it was Peaches.

As I held the phone to my ear, I could see Kane's eyes rolling in the back of his head. He was bleeding too bad so I took a towel that was nearby and tried to apply pressure to the wounded spots. I couldn't believe it, who would shoot him? Everyone in the hood knew him and his best friend, J.C., and everyone around Jacksonville always showed them love.

"Peaches, please come over here. Kane has been shot!" I screamed in the phone with tears in my voice. I knew she could tell that I was crying.

"I'm on my way, bestie," Peaches replied then hung up the phone. I knew she would be there shortly because she only stayed a couple of blocks from me. I couldn't help but cry even harder, Kane was kind, and he treated me like a queen.

"Stop crying," Kane said to me as I stroked his dreads out of his face.

I couldn't believe the man I planned to spend the rest of my life with was laying here shot and hurt. I left the church to have him, and now the same place that I ran to, was trying to take my king from me. The streets weren't for anybody, and I had no idea what I had gotten myself into. It was all happening too fast for me, and I just didn't understand it one bit. See, I'm start from the beginning of my story because this is only some of what happened.

Chapter 1

Carmon- A Change Is Needed...

I couldn't believe my parents had me at church all day once again. I loved my parents, and they had given me a wonderful life under them and the lord, so what more could a girl like me ask for? It was my last year of college, and I was finishing up my degree in Pharmacology. Yeah, your girl was going to school to be a Pharmacologist which had always been my dream. I wanted to have my own drug store, and I had already learned so much. For some strange reason, I needed and wanted more.

After church, my best friend, Peaches, came to scoop me in her new ride. She had a 2019 Mercedes Benz that was black on black, the rims were black, and so was her car, and it was nice. As she pulled up, I could hear everyone outside the church oohing and awwing. "Who car is that?" I heard one of the choir members ask.

Everywhere we went, Peaches' new ride turned heads and had people noticing us. I can't lie, I love the attention and damn sure would love a car like the one she got one day.

I loved the way her car smelled on the inside of it, yeah, it had that new car smell, so everyone knew it was straight off the lot. Myself, on the other hand, drove a red beat up 2005 Honda Accord that my parents passed down to me once I finished high school. I just stood in the door of the church in deep thought about my life. That's when I heard Peaches screaming across the church parking lot.

"Carmon, are you ready to go or what? I don't have all day now, bring your butt on!" Peaches screamed like I didn't see her standing in front of the church.

"Hold on, I'm coming!" I screamed back to her. I ran over and placed a kiss on my father's cheek and hugged my mother. "I'm gone, guys," I said as I ran towards the parking lot. I loved for the weekends to come because I knew I would see Peaches, and we would have a dope time like always.

I loved Peaches, she was ghetto and didn't care who knew it. I, myself, am more of the conservative type, very quiet, and without much to say. I guess because I would be too deep in my own thoughts most of the time, trying to block out the world. I ran to get in the car, and my favorite song was playing, A Boogie's *"Look Back at It,"* it had been a new hit of 2019, and I was digging it hard. I couldn't listen to rap, R&B, or Hip Hop music at home, so when I was out and about with Peaches, I tried my best to listen to it all. "That song goes hard," I said as I bobbed my head back and forth.

"I can tell your ass never get to listen to good music. Girl, this is this new A Boogie song, and this motherfucker go hard in the club," Peaches replied as she turned up the radio. We vibed to the beat and sung along, enjoying every word.

My father, Charles Wells, would say, "I don't want to hear nothing but the music for the Lord up in my house." Just thinking about it made me laugh. I was the only child, so imagine how bored my life had been. Having a mother and father in the church had its ups and downs, so I tried not to complain. Peaches, on the other hand, had been in and out of foster care since she was about five years old, but that's another story.

We pulled up at Peaches' crib, and it was nice. She had just moved in an apartment down town by the water with a beautiful view of the city. Jacksonville, Florida wasn't the biggest city in the world, but I loved my city.

"So Carmon, when you gon' get your own place?" Peaches looked at me and asked.

"I have thought a lot about it, but I know it will devastate my parents," I replied.

"Carmon, I know you love your people's, but you have to live for yourself, for you. You keep on, and the best years of your life is just gonna pass you by," Peaches replied, giving me a look like I needed to do better.

In Jacksonville, we used the term my people a lot referring to a person's parents, friends, and family members, which Peaches always spoke slang, and some folks would ask her the meaning to what she was saying, but not me. This was my bestie, and if nobody understood her, I did, at least for the most part.

"When the last time you heard from your boo, Peaches?"

"Who?" Peaches replied like she hadn't had a boyfriend since forever.

"You know who I'm talking about, girl, J.C., remember him, your longtime boyfriend?" I replied, giving her that look like 'girl, stop playing with me.'

"Girl, l don't even care to talk about him at all," Peaches replied, ignoring my question.

James Cook, also known as J.C., one of the most popular guys in town, dated my best friend, Peaches. J.C. was toffee colored with hazel eyes, and he had a smile out of this world. All his teeth were even which made his smile gave you chills. He was one of the biggest dope boys on the westside of Jacksonville. He stood six-foot even, and he had this swag about him that all the ladies loved. Just like Peaches got a lot of attention, so did J.C., and the ladies were flocking to him everywhere he went. Peaches, on the other hand, didn't really care; she was living her own life to the fullest, so they were off and on a lot because of Peaches' lifestyle. I never judged her, because growing up, she never had an easy life. She had been on her on since she was sixteen, J.C., on the other hand, didn't approve of her choice of a life style.

"Ok, we don't have to talk about him if you don't want to. What are we doing tomorrow, Peaches? I know you got something planned,"

"Going shopping, you already know what I love doing. We got to get us some sundresses since it's about to be summer. I want my booty to shake while I'm walking," Peaches said with a little giggle.

"Ew, you so nasty, Peaches...don't nobody want to hear about your booty shaking."

Then we both burst out laughing. I always had a good time while we were together, which made my life seem so worth it, well sometimes. She went to her kitchen and grabbed herself a wine cooler.

"Carmon, do you want one?"

"Naw, I'm ok, you know I don't drink," I replied.

"Well, I tried anyways. You know Kane been askin' about since he saw you with me that day I met J.C. over by his place," Peaches said.

"You know Mr. Wells not havin' that; he will flip if he found out I was talking to anyone hood. My father don't play, and you know this," I replied as I let out a giggle.

We both laughed so hard we had tears coming down our face.

That's what the soul needs sometimes just something simple as a great laugh just to keep the sad bugs away. When I was with my bestie, I got that, and I enjoyed every second of it. We laid around and talked for hours about everything we had missed the past few weeks we didn't see each other. We both loved romance movies, so Peaches pulled out "The Notebook", one of our favorite romance movies. It was four o'clock in the morning, and it didn't even seem late.

When I was at home, I was normally asleep by eleven o'clock at night because I was so bored. You would think I was a teenager the way my life was set up. All I could think about was how I wanted a change in my life. The only problem was I had to figure out a way to keep my parents happy. That was gonna be hard to do and still get more out of my life that I had been looking for.

Chapter 2

Carmon- The Mall...

The next morning my head was pounding from me staying up so late. Even though I didn't drink anything, I still felt as if I had a hangover. Peaches was already up and ready to head to the mall.

"Come on, Carmon, get up and get dressed," Peaches said, rushing me like she always did.

I rolled over and put my hands on my head gesturing that my head was killing me.

"Peaches, it's too early, lay back down awhile," I replied because I wasn't ready to get up.

"Nope, we got a long weekend and got to be to the beach at twelve. Besides, J.C. just called me, he asked if we were attending Duval's thug beach party they were having today," Peaches replied.

"What did you tell him?"

"Nothing, just that we would be there," Peaches said before giving me this smirk and rolling her eyes.

"Peeeeaches, I am not going. Especially if Kane is gonna be there," I replied as I stood up from the bed.

"Come on, don't ruin the day. You don't know if he's gonna be there or not. Besides, J.C. didn't say he would be there," Peaches said, trying to get me to change my mind.

"I really don't feel like seeing him, Peaches, at least not today," I replied.

After getting dressed, we headed to the mall. Peaches had a dark chocolate skin tone which was an even tone all over. Her skin would radiate when she was in the sunlight which made her melanin pop. She was on the thick side and had a bad figure-eight shaped body that would make all the guys go crazy for her. She had a perfect onion shaped ass, and whatever she wore, you wouldn't see anything but her big butt. My self, on the other hand, was a fine ass BBW. I wore a nice size twenty-two but I loved my thickness and couldn't imagine living without it. I was something that most people would call a nerd because I was book smart. Most people compared me to the singer Rihanna because of my eyes and my caramel skin complexion. My eyes were light Hazel, and I got a lot of attention because of them. Sometimes I liked the attention. Most times, not really, due to me being a really shy person; it was a little too much.

Peaches got a lot of compliments, and so did I. I personally always thought she looked a lot like the famous rapper Trina off of "Love and Hip Hop Miami." Peaches never thought so and would get thirty-eight hot with me when I would say that. She would say, " No, I look just like Peaches. Your best friend of ten years." She stayed snapping me up, but that was just how she was. She had this smart ass mouth, but trust me, she had the hands to back it all up. Peaches was known around Jacksonville for beating up bitches. That how she and I first met; she saved me from getting my ass kicked by some girls at our elementary school in fourth grade, and we had been best friends ever since that day. Peaches looked like Trina, but just know, she absolutely had her beat in the booty department. Shawty had an ass on her, and it was one of them booties you had no choice but to look at whenever she walked by you.

We ended up at Regency Mall, which was the biggest mall in Jacksonville. On a Saturday, everyone and their mother would be up in there. As we were leaving the mall, a couple of guys stopped us in the parking lot.

"Hey ladies, can we get a second of your time?"

When I looked around to see who they were, it was J.C. and Kane.

"What are you all doing up here?" Peaches asked.

"We came to shop just like you guys. Where you two beautiful ladies headed?" J.C. asked.

That's when I said, "Hi, guys."

And to my surprise, Kane was the only one who said, "Wuz up, Carmon!"

Our eyes made contact, and he immediately started smiling, blushing hard as fuck like he had been waiting on this day for a minute. He must have been happy to see me because I could feel the tension between us. The chemistry was strong, and his aura was pulling me in. From his handsome smile to his dreads, he had me mesmerized. I smiled back at him and waved.

Peaches and J.C. walked off away from where we were standing off to themselves talking which left me and Kane standing together alone.

Kane Smart, where do I start? He stood about six-foot, dark skin, muscular body with abs that would make a grown woman cry, long dreads, and a handsome and mesmerizing white smile that none of the ladies could deny. Kane was very gentleman-like, also charming but very hood, and gangster all at the same time. He had a thing for me, but I knew my father would never approve of me dating a guy like him. I had been avoiding him for a couple of months now, well since we first saw each other at J.C.'s crib January 1st, at his new year party he had which was lit. Of course, Peaches persuaded me to go, and I did. Seeing Kane that night, I knew it was something about him, but I couldn't quite put my finger on it.

"Carmon, did Peaches tell you how much a nigga been askin' about you?" Kane asked.

"Yeah, she informed me, why?" I replied, giving him the cold shoulder.

"Why you never hit a nigga up then? A nigga gave you the digits when I saw you over at J.C.'s spot New Year's Day," Kane replied, ignoring the way I was giving him the cold shoulder.

"Listen, I'm being honest, I have been busy with school. We had finals for about two weeks straight, and the last thing on my mind is calling anybody," I replied.

"Well, I'm not just anybody. It's nice to see you the type that has the beauty and the brains. I'm liking you even more hearing that news. Just don't make me chase you forever."

I giggled a little and started blushing, that's when Peaches and J.C. walked back up and asked us if we were ready to go.

As soon as Peaches and I got in the car, she started smiling.

"Why are you smiling so hard?"

"Nothing, but it seems like you and Kane were getting a little close," Peaches replied.

"Naw, it was nothing like that. We were just having a normal conversation like anybody else I would talk to. I know your ass told them we were at the mall too. You think you're slick trying to play matchmaker and shit," I replied, giving her the evil eyes.

We both started giggling.

"Carmon, I wouldn't do that, for real. They just happened to be here shopping just like we were."

"I see you and J.C. getting back on the right track," I said, giving her a big smile.

"Girl, you know he can't stay mad at me for too long," Peaches announced. She never lied; J.C. and her were on bad terms every other day.

"Where are we headed now?"

"To my crib to get dressed then meet up with the guys at noon," Peaches uttered.

"I'm not sure if I want to go to the beach. I told you I'm not trying to be all around Kane like that," I said.

"Well, we goin', and besides, you don't have to talk to him if you don't want to," Peaches uttered making it known.

She was right, I didn't have to talk to him if I didn't want to, but it was something about him that was different than any guy I had ever met before. His aura pulled me in, and the chemistry we had was crazy.

We changed into our swimsuits at Peaches' crib then headed to the beach, but we made a quick stop by McDonald's first. Once we got to the beach, J.C., Kane, and a couple of their other friends were all at the beach. They were all dressed in their swimwear just like we were. There were people in the water, others laying out getting a suntan, and a couple of people playing Volleyball.

Kane was standing over by the water talking and flirting with some chick that kind of puts me in the mind of the singer Beyoncé. She was a lot smaller than me with some nice sized hips and a cute face.

She had a polka dotted swimsuit on that was black and white. He gave her a light shove, and she grabbed him by the arm as they both fell into the water.

I'm not gonna lie, I was a little jealous seeing Kane flirting with another chick right in my face. All I could think was, *Why am I feeling this way?* Especially after all the times I had turned poor little Kane down trying to make him see that I wasn't into him.

I decided to walk over there anyway since he claimed he liked me so much. I wanted to see just how much he liked me. As soon as I stood by Kane, he jumped up out of the water. I think I startled him a little bit.

"What's good, Carmon? I didn't know you would be here at the beach today. This here is Alisha," Kane said before I could even say a word. I still never uttered a word back to him. I just crossed my arms as I stood there looking very disappointed in him.

"Alisha, this Carmon," Kane said, introducing me to her. I surely wasn't gonna speak to the bitch he was flirting with.

"Hi Carmon," she said.

Still, I just stood there a minute without a smile or a word to say.

"Kane, can I talk to you for a minute please?" I asked.

"Sure, Alisha, can you give us a minute, please?" Kane replied.

When he said that, I could tell she got upset because she was eyeballing me up and down before she ever walked away.

As soon as I knew she was gone and couldn't hear what I was about to say, I snapped off at Kane's ass. " I sure like how you were acting like you all into me, but now I see you flirting with another female. What the fuck is you doin'? You tryna be a playa or something?" I questioned with a mean mug on my face.

"Hold up, I know you ain't mad. Carmon, com' on now, a nigga gave you the digits, and you never hit me up."

"I told you why, and that doesn't mean I wasn't going to," I said in my innocent voice.

"Yo' ass confusin' the fuck outta nigga. Then your mood swings are really makin' a nigga have a headache."

"You flirting with another female not gon' make me call yo' ass any faster, is it?" I asked, crossing my arms with an attitude.

"Maybe not, but it sure got your attention, didn't it? I see you came over here. You want to be mine, just admit it," Kane replied with his cocky ass attitude. He was right though, I did like him, and I did want to be his girl, but I knew my father would never approve of us together.

I rolled my eyes and stormed off leaving him standing right there. Well, at least I thought I left him standing behind. When I looked back, he was walking and following right behind me.

Chapter 3

Kane- Compromise Love...

Liking someone like Carmon got hard at times. She is such a cutie, but too bad she wasn't trying to give a nigga like me the time of day. I had been after Carmon for almost six months now and still nothing. Most girl's in Jax was dying for me to look their way, but not Carmon. She was on the thicker side which made me want her even more. I liked my women pretty, and no matter what their size, as long as they had a big ass, I was cool, and the way Carmon's ass was sitting up in her bathing suit at the beach yesterday had a nigga wanting to smack and rub on it. Too bad Carmon wasn't that type of girl. She was the church-going type, and her father was mean as hell from what I had heard from Peaches and J.C. I tried my best to stay at a distance whenever I did see him.

Yesterday at the beach, she had a nigga's nose wide open. She had me all into her ass the way she snapped off on me for flirting with Alisha's ass, which kind of confused the fuck outta me at the same time because I had given shawty my digits a while back, and she never hit a nigga phone line. But as soon as she saw Alisha all up in a nigga's face flirting with a nigga, she turned around and got mad at a nigga then snapped off hard as fuck. I knew I could have Alisha if I really wanted to, but I didn't see her like that. Shawty was just a friend, and I had planned to keep things this way. Alisha had a crush on me since I could remember. She wasn't a bad looking girl, but she didn't have enough ass for a nigga like me. How I saw it was Carmon was gonna be my boo, and a nigga goin' all in to get her ass. She was a little feisty, but shit, I loved all that shit. I knew exactly how to handle her ass and keep her clam.

My phone rung, and all I could hear over my own thoughts was this new song by A boogie Wit da Hoodie, *" Still Think About You."*

"What's good?" I said as I answered my phone on the first ring.

"What are you up to, big head?" a girl said, but I couldn't quite make out the voice.

"Who is this, might I ask?" I replied, trying not to sound rude.

"It's sure not that chick you were flirting with down at the beach," she replied. That's when I figured out exactly who this was on my phone talking shit.

"Hi, Carmon. You finally decided to hit a nigga up, huh?"

"I guess I did, I shouldn't have. Especially after how you dissed me at the beach party for some trick with a nice bathing suit."

I could tell she was blushing by the way she was talking because it was all in her voice.

"What do we got planned for today?" I asked her, being funny since her ass had called me.

"I don't know about you, but for myself, nothing really. I got to go to church and then studying the rest of the night for my test tomorrow."

"Well, you forgot to say you have a date at seven o'clock."

"Who, me?"

"Yes, you! With a real nigga as your date too," I replied.

"And what will we be doing on this date?"

"We goin' bowling at Latitude 360. Have you ever been there before?"

"Nope, and I really can't tonight. I'm gonna call you back, I have got to go, Kane," Carmon said, and before I could utter another word, she hung up the phone in my face.

Before I could set my cell phone down good on my bedside table, it started ringing off the hook. Once again, the song *"Still Think About You"* by A boogie Wit Da Hoodie started playing.

"Got me saying, What's good with you? I remember being in a hole with you. Everything was always understood with you. Girl, I even bust a couple jugs with you. I still think about you. Girl, I still think about you."

25

I sat there for a few minutes before answering, it still blew away by how Carmon had hung up on a nigga two minutes ago.

That's when I thought maybe it was Carmon calling a nigga back, but to my surprise when I looked down at my iPhone caller ID, it read Alisha. I really didn't want to answer her, but I guess a nigga was free since Carmon playin' games. After about the fourth ring, I decided to pick up my cell phone and answered it.

"Hi, what's good?" I said as I answered my phone.

"Hey, big nose, I was just calling to see what you doin'. I'm mad bored at this house with nothing to do," Alisha's voice echoed through the phone.

"Oh, for real? I was just headed out to go bowling with some of my friends. You can come alone if you're down," I replied.

"Say less. Now you know I'm down, let's go!" Alisha said without any hesitation in her voice.

I didn't feel right going to the bowling alley with Alisha. I knew J.C. would probably bring along Peaches. Then if she was there, then Carmon most definitely would know I brought along Alisha. Peaches and Carmon were best friends, and I knew she was gonna act like a news reporter from the Channel 10 news and tell Carmon everything. I don't know why females were like that, but one thing I knew was they all talked too much. I learned that from my mother, Amoretta Smart. I would sit around for hours watching her on the phone with her girlfriends giving them the

26

run down and the 411 on what was going down in the Virginia Arms apartments. We stayed in these low-income apartments for years, and because my mother was a single parent, this was the only place my mother could afford. There would be shooting almost every day and kills on a regular. My mother always did the best she could for me and my siblings. I never judged her, and I learned so much from her about women throughout my many years growing up.

I had to bring someone alone since Carmon had turned a nigga down, I would be the only one there without a date so of course, I said yes to Alisha about coming along.

We arrived at the bowling alley thirty minutes late. Alisha took forever to get dressed, and I really didn't care how she looked, to be honest, I was just ready to have me some fun. Then, on the other hand, all I could think about was Carmon. She had a nigga's nose wide open, and I was wondering what she was doing and was she even thinking about me as much as I was thinking about her.

"Kane! What is taking you so long to get out the car?" Alisha stood outside my car yelling ready to go inside of Latitude 360. A nigga was nervous as fuck. I knew I didn't have any business with Alisha, but aye, a nigga only got one life to live.

"A nigga comin' girl, chill," I said, still not actually moving to step out of my 2019 all Grey Ferrari 488 Pista was the latest track version of the GTB Berlinetta which I had always wanted one of those when I was just a young nigga. I had promised myself once

I got the money, I would get me a fast car, and that's exactly what a nigga did.

I was nervous, so I still didn't move because deep down on the inside I knew this could possibly mess up things that I was trying to build with Carmon. At the same time, I didn't want to seem like a lame nigga on the other hand. I had homies that would clown me for shit like me sitting around waiting on just one girl who clearly didn't want me the way that I wanted her.

"Hello, do you plan on getting out the car since we have arrived at Latitude 360?" Alisha said snapping with her hands on her hips. She had made it over to a nigga's driver's door and pulled it open, waiting for me to get out.

I could tell Alisha was feeling a nigga and wanted to be seen with me. See, me and my homies were some of the biggest drug dealers on the westside of Jacksonville. We were popular and the groupies stayed ready to be down with any one of my nigga's in my crew. We had a lot of money, nice cars and the thots around Duval threw themselves at us. I enjoyed the fast life but deep down on the inside, I waited for more than just some quick fuck. In our crew, it was J.C., Mookie, King and myself. Yea, our crew was pretty small because for one J.C. was the type who didn't trust a lot of niggas. He had to go way back with a nigga to even kick it with him. We all grew up together in Virginia Arms apartments. So we all understood the struggle and knew what it felt like to live in the hood and not have shit. That was the main thing we all had in common.

Latitude 360 was a big bowling alley with all type of new technology games and luxury surround system making it seem something like a nightclub. Sunday night was always packed, and we always fell in the Latitude on Sunday's nights. It most definitely was the spot to be seen, and the whole hood would come through just to hang out with me and the crew.

As Alisha and I walked inside the place, I could feel all eyes on us. I could hear the thots whispering and saying shit, but I just ignored them. "What is he doin' here with her?" one of the chicks said.

"Girl, I don't know, but he can do much better if you ask me," the other chick responded.

That was one thing about Duval, motherfuckers stayed watching a nigga's every move. Sometimes I felt like all eyes were on me. Making our way towards everyone else, I could see J.C., Peaches, and the rest of the crew with their dates on their sides. They stood over by the check-in desk where you had to trade in your shoes for a pair of bowling kicks. Peaches was looking at Alisha up and down checking her out from head to toe mean mugging the shit out of her like she wanted to say, *"Now who the fuck is this bitch? Where the fuck is Carmon?"* She did speak to Alisha, but dry as fuck and still was looking at her sideways.

"J.C., what's good, homie?" I said once we were up to the desk.

I gave J.C. a dap then dapped up the rest of my niggas.

29

"Nun, you know, same ole, same ole around here," J.C. responded.

"It sho' is thick in--"

Before I could get my sentence out, Peaches rudely interrupted me.

"Kane, where is Carmon?" she asked with an attitude.

"Peaches chill, it's not like that. I asked her to come, but she gave ya' boy some lame excuse about studying."

"Let me call my bestie and see what she has to say about this. I done told you, you not 'bout to be doggin' my bestie for these groupies around Duval," Peaches said, rolling her eyes before she walked off.

Alisha must've felt the tension because she looked at me and said, "I'm going to the ladies' room, I'll be right back." As soon as she walked off, J.C. started giving me a lecture about bringing Alisha along. For some reason, he and her brothers never quite got along since our high school days.

"Man, why did you bring Alisha ass along?" J.C. asked, giving me a weird look.

"Bruh, I really didn't have no choice, or I would have been coming here alone. Carmon ass hasn't been givin' a nigga the time of day," I announced.

We both busted out laughing. That's when Peaches walked up and said, "What's so funny, because I don't see shit funny?"

"Nothing, we were just discussin' how your bestie turned my home boy down again," J.C. uttered.

"No, Kane. Not again." Mookie looked at me and said as he shook his head back and forward.

"Yeah, bae got a nigga hurtin', but she gon' come around," I said, reassuring everyone.

That's when Alisha returned from the bathroom, and everyone got quiet. Peaches just stared at her and walked away before anybody else even moved. That's when we all walked over to the bowling table and changed into our bowling shoes. J.C. was the first to bowl, and I couldn't believe this nigga hit a strike on his first bowl. There was not one pin left standing at the pit.

Soon as a nigga stood up to bowl and I could hear Alisha scream, "Bae, you got this." Which made my fucking stomach turn. Especially after I had told her many different times we weren't anything but friends. For some reason, she was trying to make the shit seem more than what it was, and it was starting to piss me off. I looked back at her with this disgusting look up on my face at what the fuck she had just screamed out. That's when I turned around and tried my best to focus on throwing the ball, but as soon as I threw the ball, I missed all the damn pins.

Shawty really was working hard to make these people think we more than friends. I just shook my head as I turned to walk away because I couldn't believe I had just missed all of the damn pins. I normally would strike out on my first bowl. For some reason, I wasn't too much worried about the game anymore after the little show Alisha put on. Next thing I knew, my cell was ringing. I looked down at it to see who it was, and it was my future bae, Carmon. I couldn't believe she had actually hit a nigga back up.

"I got to take this call, guys, so give me a minute," I said before walking off from the group. I could see Alisha watching my every move, but to be honest I didn't care. A nigga had been honest with her from the jump. Hell, it was up to her to still want to fuck with me.

I walked out of Latitude 360 so fast, you would have thought a nigga had won some money or something.

"Hi Carmon," I said as I picked up the phone since I knew her number from when she had hit my line up earlier today.

"Hi Kane, how's everything going at Latitude 360?" Carmon asked right off the bat. I knew Peaches had told her I brought Alisha along. I could tell by the way that she was talking.

"It's ok, I guess, but it would have been better if you were here," I uttered, trying to butter her up.

"Yeah, I'm sure. I just have a lot going on with school and everything, but I heard that you found a date anyhow, I'm not surprised since it is the same

chicken head I saw you flirting with at the beach. You must really play me for some type of fool?"

"Carmon, it's not like that. Alisha and I are just friends, nothing more than friends," I said, trying to get her to calm down.

"Look Kane, I'm not tripping, I understand. I couldn't ask you to go alone, right? We are not together or nothin', we are just friends too," Carmon replied in her calm voice.

"I wouldn't mind if you wanted us to be more, Carmon. You're all a nigga been thinkin' about these last couple of hours I been here, for real, bae," I expressed, trying to get her to believe me.

"I gotta go. I didn't call to mess up your night. Please enjoy yourself."

"You didn't though," I replied. But before I could say another word, of course, she hung up in a nigga's face. That's when Alisha's obsessive ass walked outside, claiming she was just coming to check on me.

"You good?" Alisha asked, grabbing me by my arm, pulling me close to her. I snatched my arm away from her and said, "I'm good, but I'm ready to go."

It wasn't that I wasn't enjoying my night, Alisha just wanted more from a nigga, and I just wasn't on that type of time right now. I didn't want to be here with her any longer. Carmon was like a fresh drink of water that I had been waiting on all my life, and I didn't want to mess that up for nobody. For some, I felt like I was dying of thirst that only Carmon could quench.

Once I got home to my hundred and fifty-thousand dollar condo which sat off the beach, a nigga jumped into the shower and turned on my sixty-five inch flat screen tv to one of my favorite movies called "The Notebook"; it was a romance movie--one of the best love stories anyone could watch. I know what y'all are thinking, what a hood nigga like me doin' watching a romantic movie like this? I was hood, but deep down on the inside, I was a real romantic type of nigga.

My ass fell asleep right on the sofa watching TV and thinking about Carmon's mean ass.

Chapter 4

Peaches- Bottom's Up...

Where do I start? I'm Peaches Greene, every nigga's dream girl, and most bitch's worst nightmare. I had been living on my own for a while since I ran away from the foster home the system had put me in. I had been dancing for about a year now, and I was making a killing at a club called Rock Bottom. It was more than enough for me, and I was enjoying every minute of making these racks. As you all have heard from my bestie, Carmon, I'm a little rough around the edges. Growing up in Duval wasn't easy, and living in these streets could be hell. Being a stripper had its ups and downs, but it was the only thing that kept clothes on my back and food on my table. It was nine o'clock on the dot when my thick ass arrived at work, and the club was a little dead due to it being a Monday night. The weekend had flown by, and it was another week with money to be made.

Once I got inside the club and spoke to a couple of people, I headed straight to the dressing room to change, that's when I saw three of the thots that danced with me who would always try to give me a hard time. Phat, the girl who ran the clique, she was old as dirt and had been dancing at Rock Bottom forever. She didn't like me because I had come in and was taking over all of her main customers. Which I didn't give one fuck, I was there to make money not friends. Then there was Cat and Winter, her two sidekicks who were riding with her whether she was wrong or right. As I walked towards my locker, I could hear them whisper shit about me like always. They disliked me, and I didn't quite care for them either.

"Here go Miss Think She All That," Phat said to the other two women then they all burst out giggling.

"Hi Peaches, you not gon' speak?" Cat asked.

I just looked at them because they all were so fake, and I just didn't have time for the bullshit.

"Girl, she hears you talking to her ass," Winter replied.

"First off, I'm here to make my money; nothing more, nothing less," I replied as I hurried up and changed into my club dancing outfit. Before they had a chance to say anything else to me, I heard my name being called over the intercom to the stage to perform my solo dance. I had been stripping so long that I wasn't nervous at all. I had my regular customers that came in on my nights I worked to see me, so my money was guaranteed. Growing up without a mother led me to this lifestyle, and I tried to stay clear of the snakes and fakes, women and men. After about my third dance, I went to the back and changed into my regular clothes because it was close to about two o'clock in the morning which was the time that the club normally closed on Monday nights. I made about two hundred dollars which wasn't much, but Mondays were never that busy. As I was headed to my car, one of the bouncers decided to walk with me to my car for my safety. I never worried about no one bothering me though, because my boyfriend, J.C. was well-known in the streets, and I got much respect on the count of being his lady. James Cook was his real name. He was very popular around these parts. He had always been a bad boy, but he had a soft heart when it came to me. J.C. and I had been on and off for years which was why I had a lot of love for him. As soon as I got into my car, J.C. was blowing up my cell phone like usual, so I picked it up right away.

"Hi, boo," I said soon as I picked up the phone.

"What's up, bae? Where you at?" he asked, his voice echoing through the phone.

"I'm leaving work, boo. I'm just getting off, so I'm about to pull out of here now," I replied, letting him know where I was.

"That's a bet, why don't you swing by the crib? You know a nigga needs to see you right about now," J.C. uttered, letting me know he missed me without actually saying he did. He was like a big baby sometimes but he knew I would always come when he called.

"Ok bae, give me about ten minutes, and I'll be there," I replied, reassuring him that I was on my way.

J.C. was light-skinned, tall, and very handsome. He kind of put me in the mind of the rapper J. Cole. The ladies wanted him, but he was totally into me. He didn't mind letting the world know. As I pulled up to J.C.'s house, my cell phone started ringing again as usual, but this time, it was Carmon.

"What's up, bestie?"

"What you up to?"

"Nothing much, just getting my ass off from the club, and why you still up? Your old woman ass normally be asleep by now," I replied, giggling right after I said the ending.

"Girl, I had to tell you about what Kane had to say when I called him, and I also couldn't sleep."

"Please, spill all the tea." I laughed, ready to hear this nigga's lame ass excuse for bringing that trick Alisha to Latitude 360 last night.

"He was just saying he only took Alisha's ass with him to Latitude because I couldn't come, and he didn't want to be the only nigga without a date on Sunday."

"That nigga had some nerve bringing her there while I was with J.C., and he knows I'm your bestie. He knows I was gonna spill all the tea about his ass to you. He tried it, but I bet he knows just how I get down now. Please, that hoe basic and don't have shit on you, boo." I let Carmon know I had her back a hundred and ten percent.

"I already know how you rockin', boo, but I can't believe Kane's ass. He knows how my old man is and how much he be trippin' on me bein' out late," Carmon replied.

"I bet Mr. Wells had your ass in church all day yesterday!"

"Girl, you have never lied. He was preaching for hours, and then I had to teach Sunday school," Carmon said, giggling a little with me.

"So, what you plan to do about that Kane's situation? Are you gonna give him another chance? You know Kane's ass has it bad for you."

"I don't know, one minute he actin' like he all into me, then the next minute he doin' some shit with another chick," Carmon replied, sounding like she was a bit confused about what she wanted to do.

"Girl, you will figure it out; you two love birds are made for each other. I'm about to head in J.C.'s crib, so I'ma just hit you up tomorrow."

"Ok hit me tomorrow, bye," Carmon said before she hung up the phone. I couldn't lie, I felt bad for her because I knew she really had a thing for Kane's black ass no matter how much she tried to play it off.

I had a key to J.C.'s crib, so normally, I would just walk straight in, but I decided to knock on the door tonight. He opened the door, and when he saw that it was me, he started smiling from ear to ear. He gave me a tight hug as he squeezed my right butt cheek with his left hand and placed a small kiss on my cheek.

"Why you always squeezin' my ass that tight?" I asked, looking at him with a mug on my face.

"You mean those are my cheeks, and I have a right to squeeze them," J.C. said in his sexy deep voice as he whispered inside of my ear.

We both giggled, and that's when J.C. leaned in and placed his sexy ass soft pink lips on top of mine then started tonguing me down giving me a hot and steamy tongue kiss. Just his kiss alone had me hot and ready. J.C. grabbed my hand as he pulled me up his stairs to his master bedroom. I couldn't lie, J.C.'s crib was laid; he had a big ass King-sized bed in his room.

As we entered his room, we headed straight to his bed. He took off his shirt and pants before he jumped onto the bed. He laid onto his side as he patted the other side, gesturing for me to come to lay right beside him. Once I did take off my clothes and laid down beside him, we were making out, tongue kissing some more, and rolling all around his bed. J.C started giving me small kisses on my neck and made his way down to my breasts. That's when he licked one of my nipples, sending a sizzling shiver down my spine.

My nipples on both breasts were hard as fuck. He was sucking and licking all over both of my nipples going from one nipple to the next. Right at this very moment, he had my pussy dripping wet and had me ready for more. That's when he took his index finger and slid it inside of my pussy while he continued to lick and suck on my nipples. That's when he added another finger and was finger fucking me with both fingers.

J.C knew exactly what he was doing, and I was enjoying every minute of it. That's when he moved down to my pussy and placed a kiss on my pussy lips. J.C. looked up at me and said, "Tell me you want me to taste this pussy."

He had me so weak for him, so you know what I did, right? Looked down at him and said, "Please taste me, daddy."

He licked and slurped on my pussy like he hadn't eaten in days, but I was right here willing to make sure he was good and full for tonight. He took his tongue and licked up and down on my clit, and all I could do was purr like a fucking cat. Damn, this man knew exactly what my body needed and what I wanted. His face was down between my legs for at least about thirty minutes slurping up my pussy juices. I came about three times before he got up and flipped my ass over. He pushed my back down low and grabbed both of my booty cheeks and stuck his big twelve-inch dick inside of my pussy as I gave off this big gasp trying to take the pain off it.

J.C. was blessed between his legs, and that was the main reason I was so in love with him. He had a nice long and thick dick which felt great inside of my tight wet pussy. He slapped me on the ass and said, "Now, tell daddy how much you want this dick, say it!"

Then he slapped me on the ass once again hard as fuck.

"I want your dick. Yes, I want it!"

Next thing I knew, J.C. was pulling out nutting all over my back as I let out the biggest orgasm I had in awhile. That nigga had me shaking so hard from that big ass nut that I just fell right over and laid down on the bed.

J.C. always knew just how to bring the freak out in me. Once we finished, I just laid there for a while because it was so good, I couldn't move.

"Bae, let's go take a hot bubble bath," J.C. said as he got up and headed towards the bathroom door.

"Boo, give me a second because my ass can't move," I replied still stuck.

"You need me to help you get up?" J.C. offered to come back and help me to get off of the bed.

"I got it, boo, you just go ahead in the bathroom and run our water, I'll be in there in a minute. When I finally got the strength to get up and head into the bathroom with J.C., all I could do was look around in amazement. I loved J.C.'s beautiful bathroom. It had a big whirlpool tub that you could just soak in for hours, and when I got in, I never wanted to get out. His bathroom was a his and hers type of bathroom which always made me feel right at home. After a long hot bath, we both got into his king-sized bed naked and cuddle up for a minute. J.C. had turned on the radio and put on one of my favorite songs by Tory Lanez called *"Selfish"*. This song wasn't on the hit list or anything, but J.C. loved his music which made me love it too. We cuddled for the rest of the morning until we both dozed off into a deep sleep.

Chapter 5

Carmon- Running...

Despite all the mess that had been going on between myself and Kane, I was starting to really like him. I knew I had to hide it because my father wouldn't approve of him. He gave me butterflies whenever I talked to him, and his laughter was like a song to my ears. I was home in my room just going over my bible chapters for bible study. My father always said anyone that lived under his roof, bible study was a requirement. It wasn't so much that I didn't want to attend bible study. The teacher was one of them that always spit when he was talking or reading the bible lesson of the day. Then it was a younger girl in the class by the name of Courtney Heard that got on my nerves. Her grandmother was Mrs. Heard who was on the Usher board at the church, so she was always at bible study.

As I finished Psalms 23, my cell started vibrating. It was Kane, his picture popped up on the screen of my phone.

"Yes, Kane?" I said as I answered the phone all the while stepping outside in the hallway.

"That's how you answer the phone for your future husband?"

"Nope, but for you, yep. Now, what can I help you with?"

"*Some of them caramel kisses would be nice for starters,*" Kane said in a joking manner.

"*Kiss? You know you lost it for real. Where is your little girlfriend Ashley at?*"

"*You mean Alisha?*"

"*Well, it sure looks like you know her name, so she must be your future wife.*"

"*I didn't call to talk about her. I want to talk about us, me and you,*" Kane answered.

"*There is no me and you long as you still hangin' out with your little girlfriend, period,*" I said with an attitude.

"*That's not my girlfriend. Just chill and give a nigga a chance,*" Kane said in his sad voice.

"*I hear ya' talkin',*" I replied, rolling my eyes.

"*What do you have planned for tonight?*" Kane asked, trying his best to ignore my attitude I was giving him.

"*I got bible study actually at seven tonight. You must want to come because I don't mind you coming along.*"

"Carmon, *you know a nigga like me don't do the church thing, but maybe I can take you out one night,*" Kane replied.

44

"Uuummm, I got to think about that one. You think you can just run around here with another female on your arm, and still, we should go on a date?"

"I'm not running around with nobody on my arm because I don't like Alisha the way that I like you, and you know how a nigga really feels about you, stop trippin'."

"No, I don't know, you do, but I'm call you later. I got to finish reading my bible chapters before my father come looking for me," I replied before hanging up without him even saying goodbye.

Although I wanted to talk to him longer, him lying to me about him and Alisha was starting to piss me off. Then again, I knew if I wasn't prepared for my reading tonight at the church, my father would have been looking at me all crazy, giving me that eye. It was this funny way he always did his eyes when he couldn't yell at me in front of the people in the church whenever he felt I did something he disapproved of.

Our Wednesday night church session actually flew by, and at the end of the service, I couldn't believe who was parked in the church parking lot waiting for me as soon as I came out the door—Kane. He was persistent with getting closer to me, and I just still couldn't believe he had the balls to be parked right here in the parking lot of my daddy's church. My heart dropped, how did he know where my family church was located? I looked at my pops without saying a word. I gave him a hung then kissed him, and before he could ask any questions, I told him I would be home at a distance time. I also let him know I was going out with a friend and not to wait up for me tonight. I knew the next day he was never gonna let me off easy, but I would just have to deal with him tomorrow. I ran and jumped in Kane's 2019 all Grey Ferrari 488 Pista. He had a nice ride for sure, and I couldn't wait until I could get a car that was just like it. Which I didn't know if I would ever be able to afford one, but I sure prayed that one day I would. We pulled off and were in the wind. We headed south on I-75. I didn't know where we were headed, but it felt great to escape from the church scene for a while.

"Oh my gosh, Kane, why did you come to my father's church?" I asked, looking at him confused waiting on his answer. All I could think about was that he better had a good answer.

"I wanted to see you, and I knew you weren't gonna let that happen without me just showing up, so I paid Peaches a hundred dollars for the address, and here I am," Kane said, giving me this charming smile. He had a big ass Kool-aid smile upon his face.

"You know, you can't just pull up to my dad's church like that; he gon' kill me and you. Pastor Wells don't play, and especially with you not being church going and stuff."

"Maybe he will, but spending just one night with you is so worth it,' Kane said as he grabbed my hand.

I snatched my hand away from him with an attitude. "Kane please, just drive. Where is we headed anyways?"

"We headed to the beach, just you, me, and the full moon," Kane replied so romantically.

'I'm not getting into no water, I have on my church clothes," I replied, giving him this crazy look with a little smirk on my face.

"You don't have to, just chill, please. Why you so uptight and never like to have no fun? Just live a little, you're still young, Carmon. It's nothing wrong with enjoying life before it passes you by," Kane said, trying to preach to me.

"I guess you right. Just don't get my hair wet." I utter. I had just gotten my hair done in a nice bob, and I didn't want to get it messed up.

My mind just kept rushing back to my father and what he probably was thinking right now. Kane leaned over and gave me a kiss on the forehead right between my eyes. He could be very sweet when he wanted to, but at the end of the day, he still was a drug dealer. We pulled up to the beach, and it was a little breeze blowing which made it not to cool or too hot, it was just right. Kane and I sat out on the hood of his car, and I laid back just reading the stars and staring at the moon. It was a full moon which mad the beach looking bright for it to be night time. It was beautiful, and I hadn't been to the beach since I was a little girl. Lately, my life had been filled with nothing but church and more church. Kane laid his head on my thigh. He made an exhale like he had been waiting on this moment for a while. I knew I had been pushing him away a lot, but what was a girl supposed to do when I had a father that was very overprotective and only wanted the best for my life?

"Carmon, is you gon' keep runnin' from this love I'm trying to give you?" Kane asked, giving me this puppy dog look.

"Boy hush, because from what I see, you givin' that love to everybody," I said as I started to giggle a little after I said it. To my surprise, Kane started giggling with me, and we both burst out laughing just a little harder.

"Why you gotta do me like that?" Kane asked, still smiling.

"Do you like what? That's you doin' it to yourself."

"So basically, you callin' me a whore?" Kane sat up and looked at me.

"No, I'm not. I would never call you no such a thing. I'm a Christian church girl, and we just don't do stuff like that," I replied, giving him a smirk afterwards.

"If you say so, I just want you to know I might talk to other girls as a friend, but it's you who truly got my heart. I want to marry you one day and make you my wife," Kane said as he grabbed my face pulling me close to his face. Now he was looking into my eyes, and he didn't blink not once; that's how I knew he was telling the truth. Before I could reply, he laid a passionate kiss upon my lips. I was so shocked that I couldn't move, nor could I pull away from him. He continued giving me a deep, passionate, juicy kiss, and his lips was so soft. I couldn't do anything but close my eyes as I enjoyed our very first kiss.

Chapter 6

Carmon- Checkmate...

Two weeks had gone by, and Kane and I had been kicking it on a regular. Yes, I was still getting my lessons in college, but I had started enjoying life at the same time. Things with Kane and I were official, and he was still being a gentleman like he did when we first started hanging out. He knew how I felt about getting married before having sex, and he accepted my belief. I was still a virgin, and I was twenty-one years old. I know what you guys are thinking, yes, I wanted Kane to be my first, but I also wanted it to be a special moment.

I laid on my bed trying to get some studying done, but I couldn't stop thinking about all the things we had been doing together these last two weeks. He was showing me a different side of the world, and I felt like I was officially living. His sexy chocolate face was running through my mind as I looked up at the ceiling with this big smile upon my face. Kane had me on cloud nine, and I was loving every minute he had me floating on these clouds. Just when I was about to pick up my cell phone up and called Kane to see what he was doing that's when I heard a knock at my room door. I already knew exactly who it was by the way that he knocked. "Come on in, daddy," I said just before he opened the door and poked his head in the crack of the door.

"You busy, Punkin'?" my father asked.

"Not really, I was just trying to get some studying in," I replied.

I felt like he was about to fuss at me for all the hanging out I had been doing with Kane, but I wasn't sure, so I just waited to hear what he had to say. I had been leaving after church with Kane for about two weeks now, so I knew it was coming. My father looked at me as his little princess still, although I was very much grown and over the age of eighteen. I didn't want to hear his lecture, but I was very much prepared for it.

"Carmon, who was that guy that's been picking you up from the church these past two weeks?"

"Daddy, his name is Kane. He is a good friend of mine, and I would love for you to meet him one day," I replied.

"I saw that fancy car he drivin', and no young man just working can afford to drive that kind of car. Now, don't you tell me any stories, young lady, what does this Kane, guy do for a livin'?"

"He's a banker," I said, lying to my father's face. I wanted to tell him the truth, but I knew the truth would just be too much for him.

"You really think I'm stupid, huh? You really gon' lie right to my face? Carmon, I raised you better than that," my father replied as if he knew for a fact I was lying to him.

I had no plans to tell him anything about Kane or what type of lifestyle he lived. I knew the type of person my father was, and really, no guy was good enough for me in his book.

"Daddy, just trust me. You raised me right, so just know I'm doing the right thing. He's just a friend, and there's no sin in us being friends, right?"

"You right, princess. I just don't want you to let anybody mess up your life. You have such a bright future. Listen, I'm telling you this as your father because I love you," My father replied.

"I'm good, and I'm trying my best to do things God's way. I love you, and don't worry so much. You raised a strong Christian lady," I replied, trying my best to ease his mind.

That's when he leaned down, and he gave me a tight hug and kissed me on my forehead. I knew my father wanted what was best for me, but I wanted more. Living this church life sure wasn't going to take me to those greater things in life. I wanted to have my own place and drive nice things like all the people that were around me from Kane to my bestie, Peaches.

As soon as he walked out my room, I texted Peaches.

Me: Don't forget to come by and pick me up in the morning.

Of course, she didn't reply because she was at the club making her racks. She went to the club faithfully every night. I had been talking to Peaches about helping me get a job at Rock-Bottoms. I needed to make some money so that I could get my own place. I planned on moving out soon, but I didn't want my father to know. Peaches was supposed to help me get on at the nightclub so I could make my own money. I wanted to be able to spend more time with Kane and have just a little more freedom.

I went over to my laptop and started looking up apartments in the area because I wanted something nice. I hadn't told Kane anything yet, but I wanted it to be a surprise. He would always tease me on how I was over twenty and still lived with my parents, so I was gonna show him that I was just as grown as anyone else.

Looking up apartments was only a start. I knew my father would never approve of Kane and I fully being together and the only way I was gonna pull this relationship off was get from under his roof. Even though I was getting my own spot, I planned to stay in school and work at the club with Peaches until I finished school with my Pharmacological degree. I felt like I had it all planned out; now I just had to get Peaches help and put my plan into motion.

I grabbed my cell phone, and just when I was getting ready to hit Kane up, my cell phone started to ring. I looked down at the screen to see if I noticed the number that was calling, but I didn't recognize the number, so I just answered it anyways.

"Hello, Carmon speaking," I said soon as I picked up.

"Bitch, stay your ass away from Kane," a woman's voice said.

"Excuse me, who is this calling my cell phone?"

"Bitch, you know exactly who this is. Kane loves me, and he is my man," the woman said again.

"Don't call my phone again, or I will call the law," I threatened before hanging up.

This call had me shaken up, my hands were sweating, and my nerves were all over the place. That's when my cell ring again, and before I had a chance to look at the caller ID, I just picked up the cell phone going off. *"Bitch, didn't I tell you not to call my phone no more?"*

"Carmon, it's me, Kane. What's wrong?"

"Oh Kane, my bad. I had someone call my phone a minute ago playing on my phone. She threatened me and all. Saying I better stay away from you," I replied..

"What? Who the fuck would do that? I'm coming to pick you up, and I want you to show me the number."

"I can't, Kane, my father is on to us. He just let out of my room lecturing me on the two of us."

"Wow, dang. Sorry to get you in trouble. Well, are you ok?"

"I'm a little shaken up, but I'm good," I replied.

"Well, try to get you some rest. Don't let that shit worry you. You can call me anytime you want, and I'll be right here."

"Thanks. Kane, I did have one thing I had to talk to you about."

"What's that?"

"Easter is in two more weeks, and I wanted you to go to church with me on Easter Sunday?" I asked, hoping he would say yes.

"Carmon, I'll do it just to make you happy."

Chapter 7

Kane- The Accident...

I sat in my condo watching tv like any normal night when I was at the house alone. I had just gotten off the phone with Carmon, and she was telling me that someone was calling her and saying threatening things to her. I was thinking that it could have been Alisha, but then again, I didn't really think Alisha would do nothing like that. "Martin", one of my favorite tv shows was on, and a nigga had rolled him up a fat ass Kush blunt, I was just sitting back getting high as fuck. I really didn't like smoking when I had a lot on my mind because it would have me thinking all types of crazy shit. In the middle of commercial break, my cell phone went off again, and I was so high I could hear the phone going off, but I couldn't move. I was high as fuck and stuck. Have you ever been so high that you know your mind was saying move, but your body wasn't responding? That was how I was feeling right now which I was praying that wasn't Carmon calling me.

When I finally did pick up the phone after the third call back, I heard Alisha's voice on the other end of the phone.

"Why are you not answerin' any of my calls?" Alisha asked with tears in her voice.

"I'm sorry, but I have been kind of busy these last couple of weeks," I replied, trying not to hurt her feelings any worse than they were hurting.

"You good, I was just calling to see if you had any time for an old friend? My grandmother just passed away, and I don't have any friends to talk to about it," Alisha said as she broke down in tears once again.

I hated to hear her crying, and I kind of felt sorry for her because I knew the feeling of losing someone close to you since my brother died when he was only sixteen.

"Alisha, I'm sorry this happened to your grandmother. I don't mind us talking not at all, but I do have to be honest with you about something," I replied.

"You can always be honest with me, Kane," Alisha said, reassuring me that she wanted my honesty no matter what.

"Carmon and I started dating about two weeks ago, and I know that we're just friends, but she doesn't feel comfortable with us hanging out how we used to."

"I'm your friend and have been for a while now, and I need you, Kane. Please don't leave my side right now," Alisha said, bursting into even harder tears than before.

"I'm not leaving your side. I just wanted you to know that I like Carmon and don't want to mess it up with her."

"Listen, I'm happy for you two, I am, but is it any way you can come over because I really don't want to be alone right now?" Alisha asked. Her words were ringing in my ear like an alarm clock.

I didn't know what to do or say at this moment. I knew exactly what Alisha was going through and feeling right now because when I lost my brother to a drive-by shooting, it was hard for me. I needed all my close friends and family I didn't have near me to help me pull through it. I thought about myself and the pain I endured with Rico's death and decided to take her up on her offer to come over and help her get through one of the hardest moments in her life.

"Ok, I'll be right over," I said before hanging up the phone.

***

Once I arrived at Alisha's apartment, I knew something wasn't right about me coming over here, but I ignored my gut feelings. When I rang the doorbell, I waited for Alisha to come to answer the front door. Carmon kept crossing a nigga's mind. I knew I had to keep me coming over here to Alisha's a secret, or Carmon was never gonna talk to me again.

When Alisha did come to the door, she looked very sad, her eyes were puffy and red. "Thank you so much for coming. You can come on in," Alisha said to me.

"You welcome. How are you holding up?" I asked her as I rushed to give her a hug.

"I'm not that great, friend. I loved my grandmother. She was the one person I could talk to, and she would always give me great advice," Alisha admitted as she cried on my shoulders for comfort.

"I'm here for you, Alisha," I said sincerely as I let her go from the tight hug I had just given her.

"You want something to drink? Alisha asked as she headed towards her kitchen area.

"Yes, soda would be fine. You have a nice apartment. Is this a picture of Theo and Travis when they were little?"

"Yes, that's them," Alisha spoke as she walked back towards me and handed me a cup of soda with ice.

"Thanks," I replied.

"You would never think them two was older than me."

"Yeah, they are still going hard off in these streets, huh?"

"Yes, which is leaving me to do all the funeral agreements and things of that nature by myself." We both took a seat on her all black leather sofa.

"You have your place looking nice," I replied again.

"My grandmother actually helped me decorate my apartment. She had the best taste in furniture."

"Awww, I'm sorry you lost her, I'm sure she was an angel."

After taking about four big drinks out my soda, a nigga started feeling a little light-headed and woozy as fuck. I looked at Alisha and saw about eight of her. That's when I knew I was dizzy and feeling a little faint at that very moment. My head was spinning as Alisha continued talking to me pouring her poor little heart out.

"I'm not feeling too good. Where is your bathroom?"

"It's around the corner." Alisha pointed in the direction for me to go. Before I could make it to the bathroom, I had hit the floor, and everything went black. I was passed the fuck out on Alisha's floor.

Chapter 8

Peaches- Club Night...

Friday nights were always thick in the club so I knew I was going to make over a thousand dollars tonight. The crowd was stupid thick and I was hungry for that paper.

"Peaches, you up next, so get ready," the club owner, Chip, said to me. Chip Nasty was what everybody from the hood called him. Chip was like a father figure to me. Hell, he let me start working in his club when I was only sixteen. He knew I was underage, but he also knew I was tired of going from one group home to another. I had been in and out of foster care all my life, and I was only sixteen, so I decided to start making my own money. With no work history, the strip club was my only choice, and I had to do what I had to do to get my own place. The money was fast and came easy once I got the hang of everything.

I walked on to the stage full of confidence and with my head held high because I was feeling tipsy, and I knew I was about to fuck it up. I could hear one of my favorite songs playing loud in my ear as I stepped onto the center of the stage. The song *"Rake It up"* by Yo Gotti was playing loud and clear.

"I tell all my hoes, rake it up,

Break it down, back it up,

Fuck it up, fuck it up, back it up, back it up,

Rake it up, rake it up, back it up, back it up,

I tell all my hoes, rake it up,

Break it down, back it up,

Fuck it up, fuck it up, fuck it up, fuck it up,

Fuck it up, fuck it up, rake it up, rake it up."

I started shaking my fat ass like my life depended on it which I knew my life didn't depend on it, but my bills did. I know what you guys are thinking, *Peaches, you datin' one of the hottest drug dealers in the game' so how are you lacking anything?* See, that's the thing, I hated depending on J.C. or anybody else for that matter. I liked my own money so I didn't have to worry about a nigga trying to control me or tell me what I could or couldn't do. I loved J.C., don't get me wrong, but I was an alpha female, and I couldn't be tamed. I liked to do what I wanted, whenever I wanted to.

I dropped down low and hit a split and started shaking my ass a little faster. I stood back up and grabbed the pole and twirled my ass like a windmill. I felt one guy place a bill in my thong, but I didn't stop dancing, I kept throwing my ass in a circle as I whipped my hair back and forth. I was vibing to the music and moving my body like a snake. I could hear the coward going crazy for my thick cute ass.

"Damn, shawty!" one older-looking guy yelled as he threw a handful of bills on to the stage then he slapped me on my ass cheeks. Looked back at him, I gave his ass the evil eyes, which I was looking like, 'don't you slap my ass no more.'

"I'll drink your bath water!" a guy with a Rick Ross bread screamed.

The more they screamed, the more I fucked up the stage, and I didn't have any mercy when I was in my mood to dance. That's why I wasn't that popular in the club scene. As the song came to an end, I racked up my money on the stage and made my way off the stage. As soon as I looked up, J.C.'s eyes caught mines, and he didn't have a pleasant look upon his face. He looked mad as fuck which I knew he was. I had been telling J.C. for a little over a month now I was gonna quit the stripper business. He had promised to take care of me if I quit and be with him fully. I just couldn't do it because I loved my freedom, and I wanted everything to stay like it was. I loved dancing and making own money. If he couldn't understand that, then we just weren't going to be together. I took a quick shower and changed into a skimpy ass short skirt and a pink Sprinkle Bar top. I loved my club outfits which I always got all mine custom made by a designer here in Duval. She was dope when it came to making unique outfits and that's what made me stand out in the stripping world.

After my quick shower, I grabbed my money holder and placed it around my waist so I could rakes up on more money. I had bills and they weren't going to pay themselves. I was praying that J.C.

ass had left the club already. I didn't feel like arguing with his ass either.

As soon as I stepped out of the dressing room, there stood J.C. with that same ugly ass mean mug he had on his face a few minutes ago. "So, when you plan on quittin' this shit, Peaches, as you promised me you were?" J.C. asked me, trapping me in between his armpit and the doorway stopping me from leaving his space.

"Don't start this shit, J.C. You know this is how I make my money. Hell, I have bills just like you do," I said, snapping his ass up really quick.

"And I have told you I got you. You have a man here willing to love you and take you out of this shit hole," J.C. uttered with a manager attitude.

"That is all good, J.C., but I like making my own money. I hate depending on anybody," I announced.

"We never gon' move forward if you continue to do this bullshit. I'm done if you not gon' at least try this shit my way for once," J.C. demanded.

With every word that came out of his mouth, my heart shattered into little pieces. I could feel as the little piece chipped away and filled the bottom of my stomach. At that moment, I felt sick to my stomach. I couldn't believe the words that had just left his lips.

"Really, J.C.? Really!" I screamed as a tear escaped my eye.

He had turned away from me by now and didn't utter a word back as he was walking away.

I ran up towards him walking away and hit him on his back as I started pushing him and screaming, "You never loved me anyway. Take your motherfucking ass on then!"

J.C. never turned around; he just kept walking until he made his way to the exit door towards the outside of the club. I stood at the door wiping my tears and trying to gain my composure after losing the love of my life. In the stripping business, everyone knew it was hard to keep a man, but I really didn't think J.C. would actually leave me for good.

Chapter 9

Kane- The Morning After ...

When I did wake up, my head felt like I had been hit over the head with a fucking two by four or some shit. I grabbed my head with both of my hands; it was pounding like crazy. I looked around as I sat up in what looked like Alisha's bed. What the fuck was I doing in Alisha's bed? I was confused as fuck as to what was going on. I had told this girl that Carmon and I were in a serious relationship now.

"Hi, big nose, about time you wake up," Alisha said as soon as I turned my head to look her way.

After turning my head her way, I realized that Alisha's ass was butt naked. "Wow, why are you naked? We didn't--" I asked, but Alisha cut me off in the middle of my sentence.

"Yes, we fucked, is that what you're asking?" Alisha replied with a big ass Kool-Aide smile upon her face.

"What? Noooo, I told you that I was with Carmon," I replied as I jumped up and put on my boxers and pants.

"You was the one that came on to me. You had passed out, and I was being a friend by letting you crash over here," Alisha said as she got up from the bed and grabbed her robe.

I couldn't remember anything that she was talking about. "I came on to you? I don't remember anything that happened. Last thing I remember I was on my way to the bathroom and passed out on the floor," I said in a snappy tone.

"Well, as a good friend, I put you in my bed, and once I came to bed, you were coming on to me," Alisha replied with an attitude.

"I have to go," I replied, putting on my shoes. I looked around the room for my car keys, but they were nowhere in the room.

"So, you just gon' fuck me then leave, huh? Go ahead, run back to your little church-going girlfriend," Alisha said in an angry tone.

"Hold up, you knew I had a girlfriend before you let this shit happen, Alisha. I don't know what type of game you're playing, but I came to console you as a friend about your grandmother's death, and that was it," I said as I left out of Alisha's bedroom.

Alisha rushed behind me and grabbed me by my left arm as I was picking up my car keys with my right hand from her coffee table in the living room.

"Kane, I'm sorry. You're right, I did know about your girlfriend. I just thought what we shared last night was special to you like it was to me," Alisha replied in her soft tone of voice.

"Bye, Alisha," I said as I rushed out her front door to my car.

My mind was racing as I looked down at my cell phone in my car, and I had several missed calls from Carmon this morning. She must have been headed to school because she always called me before school. I was a little pissed that I missed her call, but I had some shit to handle with J.C., so I shot him a text telling him to meet me at the spot. We had this spot that we always met up at which was what we called a bando. It was a house that nobody used, and it was somewhere off in the hood parts of the westside of Jacksonville.

Me: Meet me at the spot.

J.C.: I'm headed that way now.

Me: Bet, give me ten.

J.C. was my best friend, and if I couldn't talk to anybody else about what was going on with me, I knew I could tell him everything. Once I pulled up to the old bando, there were so many molly heads and coke heads making their way up to my Ferrari.

"You got any of that good shit y'all boys be sellin'?" a lady asked me. She had on some dirty, raggedy ass clothes with holes all through them, and her lips were all dried out and white.

"Back away from the car," I said as I stepped out of my car, making my way to the front door of the old run down house.

"I'll suck your dick for just a half piece," the lady replied.

"Look, when you come back with some cash, then we can talk. I done told you feen's don't come around here with that sex shit. We only acceptin' cash at this spot. Now bye, get your ass on!" I snapped because I was already pissed at what Alisha had done. I didn't have any idea how I was gonna explain to my girlfriend Carmon that I ended up fucking the same chick I told her I didn't want. A nigga was stuck in between a rock and a hard place, but I planned to get myself out of this hole one way or another.

As soon as I took a set at the round table in the bando, J.C. walked in the front door behind me. I jumped because I thought he was one of them molly or coke heads following me.

"Nigga, what the fuck are you jumping for?" J.C. asked me.

"Hell, I thought you were one of them damn feen's that was just followin' a nigga beggin' for a hit," I replied.

"I saw they ass outside the spot. They all over the place," J.C. replied.

69

"Man, the main reason I called you to the spot is this bitch Alisha has really lost her mind, brah. I went over to check on her because her grandmother passed away, right? How about I think this bitch put something in my cup of soda she gave me. I woke up in this bitch bed naked, and she said we fucked, but I can't remember shit," I said, pouring my problems out to J.C.

"Wow, that bitch might have given you one of them date rape pills niggas be puttin' in bitch's drinks at the clubs around here. I heard her brother Theo is pushing them roofies and selling them to people all around town. A lot of girls have been complaining about been raped these last few months," J.C. replied giving me a concerned look.

"Damn, I haven't heard anything about that, but if that bitch did something like that to me, she not gon' get away with it," I snapped.

"Yeah, I don't know if Travis has anything to do with it, but I know Theo is the one selling the shit. Alisha might have gotten her hands on some and used one on you to make you fuck her," J.C. uttered.

By now, I was feeling disgusted to my stomach just thinking about her doing that shit to me. I just didn't understand what the fuck she was thinking. If she thinks I want to be with a bitch that would do some shit like that, she was sadly mistaken.

I sat back down with my hands on my head shaking my head back and forth. I was in shock that a person I called my friend would do this to me.

"I told you to stop fucking with that bitch. If she anything like her two brothers, them motherfuckers is snakes. I never had an understanding with them two niggas, and they stay hatin' on a nigga," J.C. said.

I knew J.C. and Alisha's brothers didn't see eye to eye, but I never asked him why. Now I saw why. If they were anything like their sneaky ass sister, I wouldn't want to be fucked up with them either.

"I don't know what the fuck she did to me, but I know she said we had sex. Now I have to tell the girl of my dreams that I have slept with a girl I don't want to be with. I'm in a fucked up situation, and I promised Carmon that I wouldn't disappoint her," I uttered in sadness.

"I know what you mean. You got yourself a good girl, and I know that's hard to come by. I had to break up with Peaches ass last night. As much as I love her, she refuses to quit the stripper lifestyle," J.C. announced.

"You and Peaches will be right back together. Y'all just mad at each other right now," I replied back.

"I'm serious, Kane man, I'm sick of her dancing in that club every night," J.C. said in a mad tone.

"Look, I understand where you're coming from, but you have to look at it this way. When you met, her she was dancing, so that's just like asking her to give up a part of what makes Peaches who she is. If Peaches ask you to quit the drug game right now, would you quit for her?" I asked J.C. and waited for his answer.

"Hell no, but that's not the same," J.C. uttered.

"Why isn't it? You tell her to give up how she makes her money. No woman gon' want to depend on her man fully," I replied back.

"I guess you're right, but I'm still done with her ass," J.C. uttered with a small smirk on his face.

Everyone knew him and Peaches were off and on, but J.C. knew deep down on the inside he loved Peaches' ass. I know my friend, he was just talking to make it sound good but I gave it to tonight and he would be right back with Peaches.

"What are you 'bout to do?" I asked J.C.

"I'm about to make this play and go pick up the coke, if you can't come then it's just going to be Mookie and I. Are you coming alone?" he asked me.

"Shit, I might as well since I can't even look Carmon in the face without telling on myself," I uttered, feeling shitty for what I did behind Carmon's back. I knew I shouldn't have taking my ass over to Alisha's last night.

Chapter 10

Carmon- Avoiding Me ...

The whole day had gone by, and I only got one text from Kane. I had started feeling like his ass was trying to avoid me or something. Normally, I couldn't stop him from blowing up my phone. I had gone to class just like I always did and tried my best to focus on my classwork, but it was a little harder than usual. I couldn't stop thinking about the threatening phone call I had gotten last night telling me to stay away from Kane.

It was something fishy going on, but I couldn't quite put my finger on it. I put my book bag down and took a seat at the end of my bed and placed a phone call to Peaches. Her phone rang about three times before she decided to pick it up.

"Hi Peaches, can you come to pick me up?" I asked her even before she could say hello.

"Sure, where are you at?" Peaches asked.

"Wow, why your voice sound all hoarse? Are you ok?"

"I'm fine, just a little upset, but I'll be ok," Peaches uttered in a sad voice.

"Did someone do something to my best friend? Tell me who it is because you know I don't mind kicking some butt," I said in my playful tone trying my best to cheer her up.

Peaches burst out laughing, and so did I.

"Carmon, now you know your butt can't fight," Peaches uttered as she laughed even harder.

"I know, but it sounded good and brought a smile to your face, didn't it?" I replied.

"I'm on my way," Peaches announced.

Peaches made it to my house in ten minutes. Her eyes were red and puffy so I could tell that she had been crying.

"I'm happy to see you," I said as I jumped into her car.

"Girl, I'm happy to see you too," Peaches announced.

"Have you heard anything from J.C. and Kane ass today?" I asked Peaches waiting on her reply.

"No, last time I saw J.C. he came by the club last night flipping out on me and shit about not quitting the club," Peaches said.

"What? What was his problem?" I asked.

"He had told me to leave the club for good the other night when I came to his house, and I told him I would, but you know this the only way I make my own money, so I can't just quit like that," Peaches uttered.

"J.C. has lost his fucking mind. Like, just because he makin' money doesn't mean you should stop makin' your own money," I uttered in frustration.

"Well, I haven't heard from Kane since last night. Then on top of that, my father been trippin' about Kane and I dating, so I'm thinking about dancing at the club with you and getting my own place. The only problem is I haven't told Kane about my plan yet," I replied.

"You sure you want to move out just to be with Kane? I know you like him and all, but you have it made, girl. Living on your own is not easy nor are these bills cheap when they do come," Peaches said, warning me about moving out on my own.

"I know, that's why I'm working at the club with you. I need you to teach me everything you know about dancing so I can work at night and go to school in the day time," I uttered.

"You know I got you, girl. I'm behind you with whatever you decide to do," Peaches said, reassuring me that she had my back either way.

Once we made it to Peaches' house, I got another private phone call, and this time, my gut told me to answer the phone.

"Why you keep callin' my phone private?" I asked as I picked up the phone.

"You need to leave Kane alone before something bad happens to you," the lady said.

"Oh, yeah? How about you tell him to leave me alone," I uttered.

"I'm warning you one last time. Next time, I won't be some nice," the lady replied.

"Bitch, try me if you want to," I said in a pissed off tone.

"Who the fuck is that calling you?" Peaches asked.

"I don't know. They called me last night and just then, but both times, the number is private. I told Kane last night, but he claims he isn't talking to anybody else besides me. Only other person I know that likes him is that thot Alisha, but I don't think she is crazy enough to be playing on my phone," I uttered trying to explain to Peaches what had been going on.

"Girl, she might just be the one who is doing it. Females get crazy about a man," Peaches said.

"I haven't heard from Kane all day, but I plan to go with you to work tonight and start stripping. Can I stay with you until I can get my own place?" I asked Peaches, not sure of her answer, but I knew she would say yes.

"You know you are more than welcome to stay with me until you get your place," Peaches replied.

I was shocked but happy all at the same time. I knew I was gonna have to leave home to actually be with Kane the way that he wanted me to.

"We need to take a mall run. Since you gon' be dancin', you need some cute outfits to shake that ass in," Peaches said.

"Ugh, hush Peaches. You love saying nasty stuff," I uttered.

"I'm being honest with you, dancing is nothing easy. You have rude ass niggas with money and hating ass bitches who wish they were you. I have been doing this for a minute, and it hasn't gotten any easier for me than the first time I danced," Peaches announced.

We went to the Pink store in the mall, and Peaches got me two Pink skimpy little outfits that were cute but didn't really cover much besides my titties and ass; everything else was out in the open. I didn't know if I would be able to do this or not, but to get on my own, I had to start somewhere.

Once we made it back to Peaches', crib my cell started ringing off the hook, and guess who it was? Mr. Kane himself, blowing me up finally after he had been MIA all day.

"About time you call me," I announced when I picked up his call.

"What do you mean? You knew I was gonna call my favorite girl," Kane said in a flirtatious way.

"It took all day for you to. Anyways, what are you guys getting into tonight?" I asked.

"Who is you guys?"

"You and J.C., I mean. Sorry," I uttered.

"Oh, I don't know about J.C., but I'm trying to see my girl tonight if she not too busy," Kane uttered.

"I'm at Bottom's up with Peaches tonight. You should meet me out there," I said, still not telling Kane that I was becoming a dancer.

"Ok, I'll be out there just to see you," Kane said.

Chapter 11

Carmon- Stripper 101...

I put on one of Peaches' long, tall black jackets that covered up my whole body because I had my stripper outfit on underneath. Peaches pulled into the parking lot, and I was nervous as fuck, and coming from a church-going family I had heard my father talk bad on the club scenes and the sinners that went to the clubs. I hated that I was doing the very thing my father despised, and I felt that I didn't have a choice. It was my only way out to my parents' house and the only way I was gonna get my own spot one day.

"You ready?" Peaches looked over at me and asked.

"I don't have no choice but to be," I said as sweat popped up on my forehead. I had goosebumps all over my arms and legs. If I moved the wrong way, I felt like I would shit all over myself.

"You look sick in the face, you sure you're ok?" Peaches asked.

"I'm good," I said, lying to her because I didn't want her to think I was about to chicken out.

As we entered the club, I could see the strippers dancing all over the guys, and some of them were naked, and the others were nearly naked. Peaches and I made our way to the back of the club to the guy who owned the club office, and I could hear him on the phone with someone making arrangements for some party.

"Yeah, I told you we can have you ten girls there by eleven p.m. Sure, long as you have my money here on time, then they will be there," Chip said before hanging up the phone.

I had on a two-piece suit, so my titties were sitting up pretty, and my ass was nearly out in the back. Chip's eyes got big when he saw me standing in front of him. From the looks of things, I would say he was the type that liked plus size women.

"Peaches, my Peaches...Who is this thickness that you have with you right here?" Chip asked.

"Chip, this is Carmon, and Carmon, this is my boss man, Chip," Peaches said, introducing us to each other.

I leaned over the desk and shook Chip's hand. He turned around and placed a kiss on top of my hand.

"Damn, you somethin' pretty, and you thick with it. You gon' have these niggas in here goin' crazy. I'm just calling you Hazel since your eyes so pretty," Chip said.

"Hazel it is then," I replied without any hesitation.

"Turn around and let me see what you look like from the back," Chip demanded.

"Sure," I replied nervous as hell to turn around, but with Peaches standing right there, I knew everything was ok.

"You're perfect. When you want to start?" Chip asked.

"Tonight," Peaches replied before I could even get the words out of my mouth.

"Tonight it is. I get twenty-five percent of what you ladies make tonight," Chip uttered.

After leaving Chip's office, we ended up in the dressing room, and that's when Peaches started to tell me how the money thing went.

"I'm not telling you to drink because I know you don't, but when I get faded, it makes my night go by so much faster."

That's when my phone started ringing, and everyone in the dressing room's eyes were on me. *"Hi, I'm coming right out. Meet me by the bar,"* I said before I hung up the phone.

"That was Kane?" Peaches asked.

"Yes, they by the bar, let's go see them."

Peaches was kind of hesitant because she thought J.C. was with Kane, but when we finally made it to the bar, it was only Kane, King, and Mookie, J.C.'s crew but no J.C.

"Damn Carmon," Kane uttered after he took one glance at me. If I was close enough to him, I probably could have wiped the drool off the side of his mouth.

"Hi to you too, Kane," I said in my surprise voice as I walked over and gave him a hug.

"Carmon, these are my homeboys, King and Mookie," Kane introduced me to them.

King was a tall, light-skinned dude who kind of reminded me of Chris Brown the singer. He had a big face and a nice fade, I knew he didn't have any problems pulling the ladies. Mookie was a dark-skinned dude with a box who kind of put me in the mind of an old school type of rapper. He had the big gold necklace and some gold rings that filled up his right hand.

"Wuz up, guys?" Peaches said as she took a seat at the bar.

"I know you gon' let me be your first customer," Kane teased me.

"Sure, what kind of dance you want?" I asked, teasing him back.

"I want a private lap dance," Kane demanded

"You better have some private money too," I said with a little smirk on my face.

Peaches looked over at me and said, "You learnin' the game early, I see." Then she burst out into a small laughter.

"I'm about to head and get me a dance from that Brazilian beauty across the room," King announced before he walked off.

"Wait on me," Mookie replied as he ran behind him to catch up.

"I'm about to go give out a couple of dances and get my racks up," Peaches uttered.

Which left nobody but Kane and I standing together but alone, after they all went there separate ways. I grabbed his hand, and we made our way to the private dancing VIP room on the right side of the club. I held my hand out for Kane to give me my twenty-five dollars to even enter the private VIP for the dance.

We walked behind a black screen, and Kane took him a seat on the black leather sofa waiting for me to perform. My song had just come on and was playing by T-pain *"I'm in love with a Stripper."* As the song was playing, I was all up on Kane grinding like I hadn't been raised in the church.

"Goddamn Lil Mama,
You know you thick as hell you know what I'm sayin',
Matter fact,
After the club you know what I'm talkin bout,
Me and my niggas gone be together you know what I'm sayin',

I ain't gon' worry 'bout them really though,
I'm just lookin at you,
Yea you know,
You got them big ass hips god damn!

Got the body of a goddess,
Got eyes butter pecan brown I see you girl,
Droppin' Low,
She Comin Down from the ceiling,
To tha floo,
Yea She Know what she doin',
Yea, yea, yea,
She doin that right thang,
Yea yea yea yea ea,
I need to get her over to my crib and do that night thang,
Cause I'm in love with a stripper,

She poppin' she rollin' she rollin',
She climbin' that pole and,
I'm in love with a stripper,
She trippin' she playin' she playin',
I'm not goin nowhere girl I'm stayin',
I'm in love with a stripper."

The lyrics to the song had me feeling myself, and I was popping my ass all in Kane's face. I twirled around and dropped it down low while I had my hands on his knees. Kane was looking me straight in the eyes, and I could tell he wanted to really fuck me.

"Damn Carmon," Kane said in his deep sexy tone.

"Hush, my name is Hazel," I said, placing my finger in front of his lips.

"Hazel, can I take you home with me tonight," Kane asked?

That's when I climbed up on the sofa and stood on top of him and dropped my ass in his lap and started grinding on him harder. I could feel his dick poking the shit out of me between my legs, but I was gonna give him his whole twenty-five dollar's worth here in this VIP tonight.

Chapter 12

Kane- Obsession...

Obsession. Is one word I had a hard time learning the definition of when I was younger. Obsession is when someone who is interested has become compulsive, and they've begun to lose control over something or someone.

I never quite understood what it meant to be obsessed over nothing when my mother used to use this big word about me loving to play my game she had bought me one Christmas. My mother knew I wouldn't go anywhere without my hand game nor would I put it down for a long period of time. I'm not gonna lie, I was a little obsessed with the game. Now that I am older, I truly understand my mother's words better.

Alisha had been blowing up my phone for the past two weeks since I stopped responding to her calls or text messages since she had pulled that fuck shit on me at her apartment that night. She was obsessed with a nigga, and she wasn't back off. She called me fifty-six times in the last hour, and the more I didn't answer her, it seemed like the worse she was getting.

I was so pissed off because I still hadn't broken the news to Carmon, and now Alisha was texting my phone saying she took a pregnancy test and she might be pregnant. My life was going downhill, and it was all because of this stupid ass girl. My mother raised me to be a respectful guy, but I promise you Alisha was making me forget I had morals at all. I picked up my phone and yelled, *"Stop calling my phone you crazy, psychotic bitch."*

I was tired of Alisha, and to think she might be pregnant with my child made me sick to my stomach. I dialed Carmon's number praying to God that she would pick up.

"Hi boo," Carmon said in a soft voice as she answered my call on the first ring.

"Hi, love, I need to see you," I said

"What's wrong?" Carmon asked.

"Nothing, bae. Can you come over for a little while?" I asked, still avoiding the truth.

I knew I should have told her right then and there. It was the perfect time for me to be honest and get the shit off my chest, but I wasn't ready.

"Sure, you comin' to pick me up? Peaches not here," Carmon answered.

"Be there in ten," I replied.

Once I got off the phone with Carmon, I took me a shower. I couldn't lie, I was enjoying every second and minute of it as the warm water ran down my body. I felt the relief of all the stress

Alisha had been putting me through ease away. After I finished showering, I put on my Nike outfit which had the matching white T-shirt with the Nike check on it and a pair of Nike jogger pants which were black with the white Nike check on the leg part. I put on a pair of my black Nike shoes, and it went great together. If a nigga didn't know anything else, I most definitely knew how to dress to impress.

Getting into my car, I didn't even look at the back seat, but soon as a nigga was about to start up the car, Alisha popped her head up from my back seat, and I saw her in my rearview mirror. This chick had lost her marbles, and I was wondering how the fuck did she get into my shit in the first place.

"Hi Kane," Alisha said once I looked at her in the mirror.

"Hi Kane? It's no hi, Kane. Alisha, what the fuck is you doin' in my car?" I asked.

"I thought I would pay you a little visit since you don't seem to be answering my calls or text messages," Alisha replied with a little smirk across her face.

"Get out my car, Alisha. Whatever you think we have going on, just know it is nothing between us. I know you drugged me so you can sleep with me. Giving me a roofie still not gon' make a nigga want you. We were friends, but now we're nothing because friends don't do their friends that way. NOW, GET THE FUCK OUT NOW!" I yelled.

I was sick of her shit, and if she thought manipulating me would make me want her, trust me, it didn't. The shit she was doing just made me dislike her even more.

"I'm not going no fucking where. Remember Kane, I'm pregnant with your baby, so whether you want me or not, what do you think your precious girlfriend gon' think?" Alisha asked.

"Are you threatening me?" I asked.

"No, it's a promise. Do you think a church-going girl like your precious Carmon gon' want a nigga that has another girl knocked up? I'm sure she will leave you as soon as I tell her. Now we gon' play by my rules, or I will tell her everything, and I won't say nothing about you being drugged up while fucking me," Alisha exclaimed as she gave a little evil laugh afterward.

"You is one crazy bitch, and I wish you would just leave me the fuck alone. I don't care about you or that fucking baby. You both can die for all I care," I screamed into the phone with anger!

Alisha opened the back door and stepped out of my car, but she just stood there laughing as if I was saying something funny. I didn't know if the crazy bitch was pregnant or not, and I really didn't care. Carmon was the only girl for me, and I was lucky to have her in my life. There was no way that I was about to let Alisha mess up what I had worked so hard for with Carmon.

***

89

By the time I did make it to pick up Carmon, I was so frustrated with Alisha that you could see my veins popping up all over my body. I wanted so bad to punch Alisha's ass in the face, but my mother always taught me to never hit a girl.

Carmon was standing downstairs in front of Peaches' apartment building waiting on me to pull up since I had shot her a text telling her to be outside. I couldn't like, Peaches stayed in some nice apartments downtown, and I always wondered how the hell she was affording it.

"About time you made it," Carmon said.

"What do you mean? It didn't take me that long, did it?" I asked.

"No, I just be missing my boyfriend. I do need you to do me a favor though," Carmon said.

"And what's that?" I asked Carmon as she gave me that sexy look she knew I loved.

"I need you to take me a couple of blocks away to check out this apartment for rent. I have been working very hard to save up for it, and the landlord told me I could come look at it now. I mean, if you're not too busy, we can do it now," Carmon replied, still giving me her sexy look.

"Anything for my lady. Now stop giving me that look before I take you down through there. You be playin' with a nigga's emotions," I replied and placed a kiss on her soft lips.

"Thank you for taking me," Carmon uttered back.

"You more than welcome," I replied.

"Now, are you gonna tell me why you were looking so mad when I first got in the car?" Carmon asked.

"Dang, you notice everything. Whenever we do move in together, I'm not going to be able to hide nothing from your ass," I replied with a smirk on my face.

"I sure do, now what had my man upset?" Carmon asked once again.

"It was just some street business me and the crew were handling, that's it. Nothing for you to worry about," I said to her, lying once again.

I hated that I couldn't tell her the truth, but I was just like that. It was either I tell her and risk losing her for good, or I handle Alisha's ass until I could prove she wasn't pregnant by me. I kept thinking about Alisha being in my back seat, and I wondered how the fuck she got in my car in the first place. I shook the thought of Alisha's crazy ass off as we pulled into the apartment around the corner from Peaches that Carmon was looking to move into. I saw it was a nice quiet area, so I was at ease to know she would be in a decent neighborhood.

"What do you think?" Carmon asked.

"They are nice," I replied.

"Yeah, she not askin' for much down, but the area is nice," Carmon replied.

"How much are you asking for down?" I asked her.

"$1700, but that's with the deposit and first month's rent," Carmon announced.

"Just know I got you, Carmon. I want you to keep your money, and I'm going to pay that for you to get into your apartment," I replied.

"Kane, you don't have to do that. I have the money, what you think I'm working in the club every night for," Carmon asked?

"I know, bae, I just want you to know as your man I got your back," I proclaimed. I wanted Carmon to know that as long as I was around, she didn't have to want for shit, but at the same time, I would never stop her from living her life. If stripping was what her heart desired, I would still love and be with her through it all. Yeah, I hated her showing off her body, but I knew there was nothing I could do to stop her because at the end of the day, she was a grown woman.

Chapter 13

Peaches- Revenge...

J.C. had officially pushed me to the limit, but if he thought of me as nothing but a stripper whore, I planned to become just that. I was sick and tired of his ass judging me because of the type of work I did. Everyone wasn't blessed as he was to have a mother that actually cared and would do anything she could for him.

How I saw the thing was I didn't need shit from J.C., and if he thought I was gonna call him or run him down to be with me, he had another thing coming. At the club the other night, King was flirting with me when Kane, him, and Mookie came through, and yes, I was flirting back with him. I wasn't gonna wait another minute on J.C. to realize what a good woman I was. I planned on enjoying my life and stopped being sad over someone who clearly didn't give a damn about anybody but himself.

I looked down at my cell ring, and it was King. He and I had been hanging out for about a week now, but like I told him, I still wasn't ready to go public with our friendship, or whatever we had going on. King was sexy as fuck, he had tattoos everywhere with a pair of grey eyes, which made me go crazy about his handsome ass. He stood 5'12, and he had a cute face and put me in the mind of Chris Brown, but he definitely wasn't the pretty boy type. He was good as they come, and I was starting to really feel him. J.C. had broken my heart for the last time, and I meant that. He wanted so bad to control me, but little did he know, I wasn't going to let no man tame this ass. I made the rules, and I was going to show him why they called me Peaches.

"Hi King," I said as I answered the phone in a sexy voice.

"Where are you at? I thought we were gonna meet up today and kick shit," King replied.

"Shit, we can, but like I told you, I'm not ready to be out in the open with this shit, so we have to go kick shit in Orange Park or somewhere away from Duval. You know everyone knows J.C., and they know you one of his crew members. I don't want to start any shit between you two," I announced to let it be known.

"Look ma, he broke up with you, so if that nigga should be mad at anyone, it's himself for letting go of such a beautiful woman inside and out," King replied.

"Stop, you makin' me blush. Your ass can be so sweet when you want to be," I uttered.

I couldn't lie, I had been feeling so much better about myself since I started to talk to King. We hadn't fucked yet, but as fine as he was, I damn sho planned on letting him hit this ass. I know what you guys are thinking, I should just wait to see what J.C. gon' do, but listen, I have been down this road with J.C. too many times. It's like every time I think shit goin' good between the two of us, here he comes trying to control me, and we end up splitting up. This time, I'm doing me, and when he decides to come around, I'm already happy.

"That's what your man supposed to do for you, beautiful. He supposed to make you feel good about yourself. How about you meet me at the Orange Park bowling alley off College Street in about twenty minutes?" King replied.

"Ok, see you then, love," I said back before hanging up the phone.

I pulled in to Holley's on the Northside of Jacksonville to get me some of the best dip chicken and curly fries in all of Jacksonville. The only thing about Holley's was it stayed packed, and there was no telling what or who you might see when you were up here.

I stepped out of my Mercedes Benz, and as usual, all eyes were on me. I could tell the hoes were hating, and the niggas wished they could taste me. I swung my hair over my shoulders and kept walking until I stepped to the pickup window.

"I had a call in order under Peaches," I said to the young, cute, dread-head dude standing at the window.

"Hold on, beautiful, let me check," he said in his deep, sexy ass voice. He kind of made my pussy get wet how sexy his voice sounded when he called me beautiful.

I wanted to be the good girl that lived happily ever after with a good man, but how J.C. had been treating me lately because he

95

couldn't have things his way was outrageous. I rather be alone before I let a nigga think I needed his ass, and I meant that.

"Thank you," I said as he handed me my bag of food.

As soon as I turned around to walk away from the window, I saw Alisha's ass walking towards me. She was the last bitch I wanted to see since she had been trying to get my best friend's man.

"Well, if it isn't Peaches, J.C.'s girlfriend," Alisha said in a chimmy way as she approached me.

"And if it isn't Alisha, the sideline whore who been tryna get with my best friend, Carmon's boyfriend, Kane," I said with an attitude. I was ready for this bitch to come back with some words that would make me get off in her ass right here about Carmon and Kane if I had to. I was already frustrated about the J.C. bullshit, but I would gladly take all my anger out on this bitch if I had to.

"Sideline whore?" Alisha said as she chuckled about three times.

"Yes, that's what we call bitches who want someone else's man that isn't her own," I replied.

"Oh, I'll be that, but please let your precious friend, Carmon, know that I'm pregnant by her so-called man," Alisha replied then chuckled again before I could say another word back to her.

I didn't believe that bitch about being pregnant because I knew how these Jax thots could be. They would holla pregnant as soon as they realized the nigga ain't fuckin' with they triflin' asses no more. See, J.C. had a couple of bitches that claimed he was the father of their kids, but he always wasn't when the DNA test did come back.

I knew how it was in these streets, and bitches like Alisha would do anything or say anything to make a nigga be with them.

I jumped in my Mercedes Benz and turned my music up high and started singing one of my favorite songs by the city girls called "Clout Chasing."

"Told that lil' bitch stop clout chasin' (Clout chasin')
Told that lil' bitch that I'm not basic (Not basic)
Pull up on that bitch and put them hands on her,
(Doo, doo, doo)
If she keep cappin', then I'm layin' on her,
(Ooh, ooh, ooh)
Told that lil' bitch stop clout chasin' (Clout chasin')
Told that lil' bitch that I'm not basic (Not basic)
Pull up on that bitch and put them hands on her,
(Doo, doo, doo)
If she keep cappin', then I'm layin' on her,
(Ooh, ooh, ooh)
Told that lil' bitch stop clout chasin' (Clout chasin')
Told that lil' bitch stop clout chasin' (Clout chasin')
Told that lil' bitch stop clout chasin' (Clout chasin')
Told that lil' bitch stop clout chasin' (Clout chasin')."

Alisha's ass most definitely was a clout chaser. She didn't have anything going on; the bitch let her brothers take care of her while she sat at home doing nothing just thinking she was pretty but was a dummy. I knew she told me that information so I could take it back to Carmon to break Kane and Carmon up, but I wasn't even telling Carmon shit about her dusty ass. She's lucky I was trying to go meet up with my new boo, or I would have beat her ass right there in front of Holley's.

Before I got to the blowing Alley in Orange Park, I had already finished eating my Holley's and was feeling full as fuck. That was one thing about me, I was going to eat up some shit because all my weight went to this big ass and my hips. I didn't work out at all, but my figure-eight body made it look like I did.

I could see King from where I was parked as he stepped out of his red and black 2019 Camaro with his outfit to match--my heart started to flutter. I couldn't lie, I had always noticed King watching me since high school, but I never thought to give him the time of day, but now, I was kind of glad I did. King walked his handsome ass up to the window of my car and said, "Get your fine ass out so I can see you."

"Hold on, let me fix my lips. I stopped by Holley's and grabbed me something to eat and messed my shit up," I uttered, still looking in my mirror applying some lipstick to my big, full, sexy ass lips.

"I don't know why you puttin' on that lipstick because you know I'm gonna lick all that shit off, right?" King replied in his sexy tone.

"Oh yeah, I hear ya' talkin'," I replied as I gave him a little smirk, stepping out of my car.

As soon as I got out, King placed his arms around me and hugged me tight as he squeezed my right ass cheek.

"I always wanted to do that," he said as he grabbed my hand and placed a kiss on my left cheek.

Chapter 14

Carmon- The move in...

Kane helped me to get my apartment like he said he would, and now it was my move-in day. A month had gone by, and I had finally gotten up all the furniture I needed. Now the biggest thing was going to be my parents, how facing my father after I had been gone from home for so long would be. I couldn't face him because I knew what he was going to say. Kane was the devil, and I was letting the devil control me since I wanted to live my own life.

"Peaches, can you drive me to my parents' house to get the rest of my things please?" I said, calling out to my best friend.

"Hold up, I'm coming!" Peaches screamed.

She must have had a hangover because that's the only time she would scream when she did. I screamed back at her and said, "Come on, you know I'm trying to be in my new place this weekend."

I decided to leave my 2005 Honda with my parents and to just get my own car. I wanted something up to date that looked nice. I had a few more weeks left in school, and I planned to be driving something nice once I had my Pharmacology degree in my hand.

Peaches finally got her butt up, and we were now headed over to my parents' house so I could get my things and say my goodbyes. I already knew my father was mad by the text he sent me for not making it to church on Easter Sunday. Every year, I read a scripture out of the bible to the church and help the little kids find eggs. I was so busy with getting my own spot that Kane and I decided to do something together, so I didn't make it. Kane told me he wasn't comfortable going to my father's church after I told him my father didn't want me dating him about a month and a half ago now. I didn't blame him for not wanting to be around someone who wasn't even willing to give you a chance as a person, not just a drug dealer.

Pulling up to my parents' home, I felt a chill come over my body. I knew something was about to happen, I just didn't know exactly what it was.

"You coming inside with me?" I asked Peaches.

"Girl, no, you know how irritated I get when I have a hangover," Peaches replied.

Peaches had been drinking a lot harder since J.C. and her split up, but it wasn't my place to tell her to stop. She was grown, and grown people had to make their own decisions; that's what my father used to tell me. Well, that just meant in my father's eyes, I wasn't grown because he hated when I made my own choices, period.

"Ok, I'ma just run in there and come back out. Don't leave me either, Peaches," I said, warning her.

"I'm not going to leave you," Peaches uttered with a smirk on her face.

One thing I knew was Peaches hated waiting on anybody and would leave me if I took too long. I got out of Peaches' car and made my way to my parents' front door. I rang the doorbell as I prayed to God that my father wasn't home because I just wasn't in the mood for his preaching right now. My mother came to the door, and she gave me a big smile whenever she did open it.

"Oh my God, it's our baby girl, Charles!" my mother yelled out to my father to come to see.

As always, my mother took me in her arms and embraced me like she hadn't seen me in years. I loved my mother, but sometimes, she was just a little extra with everything.

"Ma, please," I pleaded trying to get loose from her tight arms around me.

"Baby, I just really miss you. Have you been eating your vegetables as I told you to?" my mother asked.

"Yes, Mama, I have," I announced back.

My father finally made his way to where we were standing and stopped about a foot before getting to where we were.

"I see you have come back. I hope it's for good because God isn't pleased with what you're doing, young lady," my father continued to preach to me.

"Daddy, I only came to get some more of my things. I've gotten my own apartment, and I'm ready to live my own life," I explained.

"Carmon, get everything you think you might need," my mother stated.

My father just dropped his head and walked away. I knew he hated me being away from his house, but I needed to see what the world was about without my father and mother guiding me every step of the way. I knew kids without parents wished they had some exactly like mine, but I just wanted to be free. Free to love who I choose, free to be an adult without breaking my parents' rules, and free to live my own life that was not theirs.

Once I had all my clothes and had gotten back inside Peaches' car, I let a tear fell from my eyes. I really wished that my father would just accept Kane for who he was, but my father just wasn't that type of person. He only wanted the best for me, and I knew that deep down inside. If only I could get him to understand that Kane was what was best for me. At least I thought he was what was best for me, and besides, he had been more than generous to me. He not only helped me get in my apartment but funded all the money I needed for my furniture as well. How I felt, I couldn't ask for a better boyfriend.

***

Once we had made it back to Peaches' place, my cell was ringing, and of course, it was Kane. I looked down at my phone as Ace Boogie wit da hoodie song *"Look Back at It"* played. That was one reason I was happy as hell to be away from my parents' house. Now I could play any type of music that I liked to without my father making me feel bad or tell me it was against his house rules.

"Hi bae, where have you been?" I asked.

"I have a surprise for you," Kane announced.

"A surprise? What kind of surprise, Kane?" I asked.

"How about I come over to show you?" Kane replied.

"Ok, if you insist. I was just about to head to the apartment so I could put up all my clothes and things," I stated.

"Then I just made perfect timing then because I can help you," Kane said.

"Sure, I'll see you when you pull up," I said before hanging up the phone.

Once Kane pulled up in his Grey Ferrari I saw his friend Mookie pulling up behind him in a dark purple and black Jeep. I couldn't believe my eyes, but Kane had purchased me a purple jeep wrangler 2019. Wow, that baby was beautiful too, and it was just like the one I had told him I always wanted. I felt beyond blessed to have a man that not only listened but was set on making my dreams come true. Kane stepped out of his car and ran up to me with keys in his hand.

"Bae, look what I got for you," Kane announced.

"Aww boo, you shouldn't have," I stated, but deep down on the inside, I was more than grateful.

"Bestie, I see you, girl," I heard Peaches uttered from behind me.

"Isn't she nice?" Mookie stated.

"She is beautiful and exactly what I wanted," I said, rushing to look on the inside of my new vehicle that my boyfriend had bought me.

Peaches' ass ran right behind me and stated, "I hope I get to drive it after you do."

I looked at Peaches and burst out laughing because she always did say the first thing that came to her mind.

Chapter 15

Peaches- The Throw Down...

Here we go again, it was another night in Bottom's Up, and I wasn't in the mood for nobody bullshit. King had been MIA and not to mention J.C.'s ass was still on some fuck shit. I entered the locker room to get dressed so I could get changed to make me a little money before it got too late. It was a Friday night, and Carmon hadn't come in yet. She had called me about thirty minutes ago saying she was on her way in, so I decided I would come in, dance, and kick shit with my bestie for a little while.

As I entered the dressing room, Phat was sitting her ugly ass up on the table where we put on our makeup under the mirrors, with a beer in one hand and her cell phone in the other.

"I guess it's time to go since the dressing room gettin' a little crowded," Phat stated under her breath like I didn't just hear every word that came out of her mouth.

"Phat, your ass is so crazy," Cat uttered cheering her on.

"Let's just head to the dance floor," Winter said.

"Yeah, it is a little too crowded because your ugly ass is in here," I said with an attitude.

"Ugly! That's one thing I'm far from, bitch, but if you got a problem, I'll be happy to solve that for you," Phat stated in a mad tone.

That's when Carmon entered the dressing room and ran to stand in front of me trying to calm me down.

"Bitch, you know what it is," I said, ready for whatever she wanted to do. I was sick and tired of their shit, and I had enough of them picking on me for no fucking reason.

"I'm gonna show you just where your bitch is at!" Phat screamed out as Cat and Winter pulled her out of the dressing room.

"You the only ugly bitch I see!" I screamed back at her as Carmon stood in front of me.

"Wow, what in the hell is going on?" Carmon asked me.

"Nothing," I said as I snatched my arm away.

"Oh, it is something. Why are you trying to fight Phat and her clique? You know we have had this talk before, best friend. They are just miserable bitches, and misery loves company," Carmon stated.

"I know you're right, but I'm sick of their shit. I come into this motherfucker to make my money, and that's it. But I'll be damned if I'm gonna keep ignoring them ugly ass bitches," I screamed with tears in my eyes!

"Look, I know it's hard, but you better than that. You're only here to get your money and go home. We not gon' be doin' this shit long. Once I get my degree, I'll help you go back to school even if I have to come to class with your ass," Carmon said with a smirk on her face that made me burst out laughing.

I loved that about her, she always knew just what to say to make me laugh. Carmon had a good head on her shoulders, and she kept me leveled.

"I know you right. I just need to get me a drink and relieve some of this stress," I stated.

"What is wrong with you, best friend? You know you can talk to me about anything," Carmon said.

"I just know I have fucked up. I haven't told you because I didn't want you to be involved if shit goes left. I started seeing King's ass, but now he has been acting funny towards me. Not to mention, I haven't heard from J.C. in about two months now that we're not together. Shit just crazy as fuck for your girl right now, bestie," I announced.

"Damn, I thought my life was about crazy right now with me moving out, but you got me beat. So when was your ass gonna tell me about you and King? Girl, I'm just saying this, J.C. is a little crazy looking. You sure he not gon' try to kill the both of you?" Carmon asked.

She was right, J.C.'s ass wasn't wrapped too tight in the head. "He broke up with me. I'm sick of him just dropping me when he gets ready to and thinks I'm always gonna be around whenever he is ready to pick me back up. I know my lifestyle is not ideal, but neither is his life. He is a drug dealer which is fast money just like stripping is," I explained, trying to get Carmon to see shit from my point of view.

"I understand where you're coming from. Have you tried to talk to J.C. about what he is doing and how you feel?" Carmon asked.

"Nope, I'm not trying to call nobody and talk to them if they aren't trying to call and talk to me first," I uttered.

"When you love someone, Peaches, you have to stop being selfish. Let your pride down and be the bigger person to truly be happy," Carmon said.

"I get what you sayin', Carmon. I'm just done with him coming in and out of my life," I stated.

"Well, only you know when you have had enough. Now let's finish getting changed so we can go and shake our asses for these racks," Carmon replied.

After we got dressed, I could hear my song playing "Twerk" by the City Girls ft Cardi B, and I was ready to shake my ass until I felt better about my nigga's acting up on me.

"Work that (I want a slim, fine woman with some twerk with her)

Work that (I want a slim, fine woman with some twerk with her)
Please (I want a slim, fine woman with some twerk with her)
Make 'em dance, twerk (twerk-twerk-twerk-twerk-twerk-twerk with her)
Twerk, twerk,
Twerk, twerk,
Twerk, twerk,
Twerk,
(Turn the lights off!)"

Once we were dressed fully, I ran out of the dressing room so I could dance, and you won't believe who I bumped into on my way out of the dressing room. Phat's ugly, old, dirty-looking ass.

"Excuse you, bitch," Phat said before I could say excuse me.

"Bitch," I uttered back, then I hit that old bitch right in her left eye before she could say another word.

"Noooo, Peeeaaches!" I could hear Carmon scream as she tried to grab me.

I snatched my arm away from Carmon and punched Phat in her face once more then she hit the floor. Now I was on top of her punching this old bitch in her face because she deserved it. I was sick of her shit, so I made sure I taught her ass a lesson.

"Get your ass off of me, bitch!" Phat screamed.

"I'm gonna show you exactly what a bitch can do!" I yelled as I punched her one last time in her head.

"Get her up off of her!" Cat screamed as she stood next to us fighting.

"She gon' kill her," Winter screamed!

That's when I felt one of the security guards pulling me up off of her, so I kicked her dead in the face with my heel which landed dead in her right cheek. I had put a hole in that bitch's face with my heel, and I didn't feel bad about it either.

"Put her down!" I could hear Carmon screaming at the security guard.

"Not until she is outside of this club," he said.

Now we both were outside of the club and couldn't make our money for tonight.

To Be Continued...

WHAT MAKES YOU UNIQUE:

Reaching for your goals no matter who doubts you is what makes you unique. Not letting this world take your creativity and remaining humble no matter what causes you to stand out. When life gets tough, don't give up, just keep pushing for the stars. The people that shine the brightest are often the ones who have been down the darkest roads.

About the Author

Lashay Perkins, pen name is Uniquely Lashay, has a degree in Health Care Administration, works full time in the medical field, and she is a part- time writer. She wants to further her future in writing full time. She is a mother of three kids and two dogs; one is named King, and the other one is named Prince. She loves to write in her free time. She lives in Bainbridge, Ga but has also resided in Jacksonville, Fl for the past ten years. Writing and reading have always been a joy for her since she was a child. She enjoys telling stories for the curvy women around the world. It has always been her pleasure to share her view on the world. Writing has always helped her to escape from her everyday reality. She hopes her work is enjoyable and entertaining.

Keep In Touch with Uniquely Lashay....

Facebook: @Uniquely Lashay

https://www.facebook.com/profile.php?id=100027014030850

Instagram: @fancyshay1

https://www.instagram.com/fancyshay1/

Twitter: @fancyshay

https://twitter.com/fancyshay1

Wattpad: @fancyshay1

https://www.wattpad.com/user/fancyshay

Author Page: @AuthoressUniquelyLashay

https://www.facebook.com/AuthoressUniquelyLashay/

(Facebook) Promotion page: @Unique Creations book Promotions

https://www.facebook.com/groups/2028167847297707/

Interview By OG Publications

http://www.ogpublications.com/interrogation-room-meet-author-lashay/

Interview By Voyage Magazine

http://voyageatl.com/interview/meet-lashay-perkins-uniquely-lashay-currently-live-bainbridge-ga/?fbclid=IwAR1rQqNxTJFTVGMyfmwpJZJC7Awe-WmXR1LkaXWUYkmycfWDtB-VxgnUyaI

Looking for a Publishing home? Hit us up if you are looking for a family, not just a business. Let us show you the real meaning of publishing with love, respect, and hard-work. We accept experienced and aspiring writers. We will give the aspiring writers guidance and mentoring to make it in this industry.
(Unique Creations Publications) *is now accepting submissions in all genres.*

uniquecreationspublication@gmail.com

CPSIA information can be obtained
at www.ICGtesting.com
Printed in the USA
LVHW082153140220
647003LV00012B/327